THE FIVE SISTERS
POWER

JONAH'S POWER

THE FIVE SISTERS POWER

TaQuanda Taylor

TaQuanda Taylor

2014

Copyright © 2014 by TaQuanda Taylor

First Printing: 2014

ISBN 0692294031   ISBN-13: 978-0-692-29403-1

Dedication

This book is dedication to my grandmother and biggest supporter. I wish you were here to see this all happen but I know that you are proud of me. I miss you everyday and I love you. Thank you for being you and for loving and supporting me.
Martha Taylor
1946 – 2013

Table Of Contents

Acknowledgements

I want to acknowledge everyone who supported this journey to complete this book. I know you guys have been waiting and I thank you for being so patient with me.

Chapter 1: Genesis

Genesis let out a sigh and glanced at the time on the dashboard. *4:59.* It was almost five o'clock in the morning and Genesis had been driving around all night. She lived in the coveted 'City That Never Sleeps' yet it had been awfully quiet. She only had one call to answer and it was for a minor domestic disturbance case, which the two parties decided to solve themselves. She hated being bored.

Genesis Battle was 29 and a New York City Police Officer. On most nights she liked her job. Maybe even loved it, especially in this city. There always seemed to be something going on. Tonight, however, there was nothing. She was bored and anxious at the same time.

She stared aimlessly out the window. She stared at her reflection in the side view mirror. Her normally bright green eyes looked dull and tired. Her mocha complexion looked pale. She couldn't remember looking this tired before.

The way she looked coincided with the fact that she had a weird feeling. She didn't know how to explain it. Her spirit felt uneasy. She felt like something was going to happen yet she couldn't put her finger on it.

"Are you okay?"

"Yeah," she answered. She turned to look at the man sitting next to her driving.

TaQuanda Taylor

Sergeant Chris Helms was a handsome man of 35. He had recently been promoted and Genesis couldn't be more happy for him. She felt lucky that she got to continue to ride with him. She didn't feel pressure because he was the boss, like many would. He was her friend and she was honored to be able to ride with him.

"You look like you were somewhere else," Chris said with very clear concern in his voice.

"Just tired is all." Genesis wasn't sure if Chris would understand her if she told him what she was feeling. They were friends but that didn't mean he wouldn't think she was crazy.

Ten years ago, when she was 19, she became the sole guardian of her four younger sisters. She had put her dream of becoming a lawyer on hold when they needed her most. The college credits that she had acquired gave her the chance she needed to enroll in the police academy and she was partnered with Chris.

At the time it seemed like the best way to make enough money so that she could take care of her and her sisters. Now she had to admit that she actually liked the job. She worked the night shift while the older two were home with the younger two. That way she was able to be home when the younger two got out of school.

It wasn't a perfect system but it worked for them. Over that time Chris had become a good friend of hers. Although he wanted more.

Chris' phone chimed that he had a new text message.

With raising four girls she always found herself checking cellphones to ensure that everything was on the up and up. She felt like that was something a parent would do. It was such a habit that she couldn't help but look over at Chris' phone.

The moment she saw the image on his screen she regretted it.

"Seriously?"

"What?" Chris looked over to see what she was talking about. Realizing that she saw the picture, he locked his phone. "That's what you get for being so damn nosey."

"I'm sorry. I didn't expect you to be sexting."

"Well, I need some entertainment. It's dead tonight. Unless you were planning to entertain me."

"In your dreams."

"Always."

Genesis laughed at the joke. She always laughed when he talked like that because she never believed that he was serious. She took their friendship very seriously and she believed he felt the same way.

"You're 35 years old. I think it's time to stop sexting."

"Never." He attempted to sound serious. Genesis hoped that he was not serious. There were so many other things he could be doing with his time.

"Whatever. Can you find someplace to stop? I have to use the bathroom."

"I think there's a bush around here somewhere."

"I am not using the bathroom in a bush."

"Okay Miss. High Maintenance," he said jokingly.

Chris pulled into the parking lot of McDonalds on Flatbush Ave. It was his favorite place to eat so Genesis wasn't surprised when he chose there to stop. She was sure that if she hadn't said something about needing a bathroom he would have stopped there eventually.

TaQuanda Taylor

He stopped the car by the front door and they both climbed out. They stepped up to the door and Chris knocked. The place was pretty much shut down except for the drive-thru.

They waited for someone to let them inside. Genesis peered through the glass, sure she saw someone moving in the back. She hoped someone was on their way to open the door.

She began pacing back and forth away from the door. She was sure she was going to have an accident if someone didn't come to the door soon.

Chris knocked again and she stepped away from the door. Something made her turn and look towards the drive-thru.

She couldn't believe what she was seeing.

A man climbed out of the small window.

"Hey!" Genesis called out.

The man hit the ground and turned to look at her. Chris backed away from the door to see why Genesis had called out. The man turned and took off running in the opposite direction. An employee ran to the door and unlocked it. Chris ignored him and ran to the car.

Genesis didn't know why but instead of getting in the car, she took off on foot after the guy.

The car was right there and it would have only taken a few seconds for her to get to it but the same feeling that told her to look at the drive-thru window was now telling her to run.

"Genesis!" Chris called out her name.

But she couldn't stop.

—

She could hear the car door slam shut and the engine start up. The man had a little of a head start and Chris would probably catch him before she did.

Genesis made it to the street and chased after him. He was pretty fast. She couldn't help but think that he had probably ran track in high school. Maybe he could have had a career as a cross-country runner.

The man sprinted down the street. She pushed herself with everything she had to keep up. It felt like her legs were going to give out from under her. It was taking everything that she had to keep up with him.

She felt like passing out but then the feeling quickly faded away. She suddenly had a surge of energy.

The man made it around the corner. Chris sped past her and he too made it around the corner. She knew he would get to him first. *Why didn't I get in the car?*

She heard the shots before she made it around the corner. Chris swerved the car to avoid being hit. The front of the car crashed into a light pole.

She turned to find the man. He was standing, aiming the gun at the car. Genesis reached for her own gun but she wasn't quick enough.

He turned the gun on her and fired two shots.

Genesis felt the bullets hit her. She was shot in the chest, the bullet narrowly missing her vest, and then in the right arm.

It felt like nothing she thought it would feel like. She had never been shot before but she expected to be in severe pain. Yet, she barely felt the bullets.

TaQuanda Taylor

The man turned and continued running. She saw Chris jump out of the car and run towards her. She had two choices to make. Stay or go.

Without really thinking she chose the latter.

She could hear Chris yelling her name as she took off down the street.

She didn't know how she was able to run after being shot twice but she was beginning to pick up speed. She was quickly closing the gap between them. He looked over his shoulder and surprise flashed across his face. She felt a little joy out of that.

He took his gun out and fired at her again. She was hit in the right leg. It slowed her down a bit.

He turned and ducked into an abandoned building. She ran in after him. She stopped right inside the entrance to see where he had gone. She could hear him and looked up. He was running up the stairs. Without a second thought, she took off after him. He fired the gun over the banister.

The bullet hit her in the left arm. She continued up the stairs after him.

The man stepped onto the landing of the third floor and she was right behind him. She reached out to grab his arm and was surprised when he spun around.

Before she had a second to react, she was punched in the face. She felt her head bob back. Instinct took over.

Genesis had never been in a fight before but she knew that she had to defend herself. She threw a punch as hard as she could.

Crack

6

The sound made her think that she had broken his jaw, but that was impossible.

He screamed out in agony. Genesis reached for her handcuffs. If he really did have a broken jaw she would have a lot to explain.

Distracted, she didn't notice that he had regained most of his senses.

He backhanded her across the face.

Damn, that was a rookie move, Genesis.

She stumbled and almost fell down the stairs. She reached out and grabbed a hold of the railing to steady herself. The man moved towards her and all she could think about was getting him away from her. Genesis kicked out and he stumbled back.

Genesis moved farther onto the landing making sure that she was nowhere near the stairs. She couldn't imagine taking that fall.

She was grateful that she didn't fall but she needed to pay attention to the task at hand.

They stood on the landing fighting for what felt like hours to Genesis, but it may have only been minutes. He managed to back her against the banister and wrap his big beefy hands around her neck. It felt like her windpipe was being crushed. She punched and kicked with all of her might trying to get him off of her.

He wouldn't let go.

As he pressed her against the banister, she could feel it loosening under their combined weight. She needed to get him off of her before they fell. Doing what girls did best, she scratched at his face and managed to scratch him across the eye.

He screamed out in pain. That didn't make him let go. What happened next seemed to happen in slow motion. He raised his fist

TaQuanda Taylor

and punched her three times in the face.

That was it. The banister couldn't take anymore.

If she was going to fall, so was he.

She grabbed onto his shirt and they fell three stories crashing to the floor.

Genesis winced in pain as she opened her eyes. There was pain radiating through her entire body. She felt like she had been hit by a truck. But she was doing better than the other guy.

The man was lying not too far from Genesis in a crumpled mess. Genesis was on her back and the man was on his stomach. She wondered if he was still alive and then he started to stir.

"Freeze!"

She turned her head and saw Chris standing in the entrance to the building. His attention and gun were focused on the guy. He turned his attention to Genesis.

"Are you okay?"

"Yeah."

Chris turned his attention back to the man. Genesis followed his gaze.

"What about him?" she asked.

Chris walked cautiously over to him. He bent at the waist, never taking his gun off of him, and checked for a pulse.

"He'll live."

"Good." Genesis remained where she was and focused on the man. "You have the right to remain silent. Anything you say, can and will be used against you in a court of law. You have the right to an attorney. If you cannot afford one, one will be appointed to you. Do you understand these rights as I have read them to you?"

The man let out a barely audible grunt. Genesis wasn't sure if it was in response to her or not. She turned away and looked up at the ceiling. The pain in her body was beginning to subside. She knew that she shouldn't be recovering so quickly.

Genesis was trying to figure out what was going on when two police officers entered the building with their guns drawn.

"We're going to need two stretchers in here," Chris said.

"You only need one. I'm fine," Genesis objected. She started to sit up. Before she could object more, one of the officers left the building.

"Genesis don't move," Chris said.

"I'm fine. Really." Genesis attempted to get up again.

"Genesis don't make me pin you down," Chris said.

I'd like to see you try. The instant Genesis had the thought she laid back down.

The other officer walked over to Chris with his gun trained on the man. Chris put his gun away and removed his handcuffs. He put them on the man and began to carefully search him.

Genesis watched him with her earlier thought running through her head. She wasn't a violent person, not normally, but when Chris had threatened to pin her down, she had wanted him to just so she could prove he couldn't. She felt oddly competitive.

—

TaQuanda Taylor

Four paramedics and the other officer entered. They had two stretchers with them. Two of the paramedics walked over to Genesis and knelt beside her to check her over.

"I'm fine."

"She fell from the third floor," Chris interjected.

"Does he have ID on him?" Genesis asked, trying to change the subject.

"Yeah," Chris said. He opened a wallet he was holding and took the ID out. "Name is Mark Washburn. He also had this bag of money and this gun."

Chris mentioned the gun and stared at Genesis. She was sure that he was thinking about the man shooting at her and wondering if she had been shot. She was still trying to figure that one out. The paramedics try to get her onto the stretcher.

"What's your name?"

"Mario." The paramedic to her right responded.

"Listen Mario, I'm fine. You can go."

Mark is loaded onto the second stretcher and carried from the building. The two officers follow behind.

"She's going to Beth Israel," Chris said.

"Can I at least walk?"

"No." Chris responded.

Genesis wanted to argue with Chris about how she was capable of walking on her own two feet but she knew that it would do no good. He was her superior and if he said that she had to get on the stretcher and go to the hospital then that's what she had to do.

Genesis scooted onto the stretcher and laid back. The paramedics picked her up and carried her from the building. She knew the trip was pointless but kept her mouth shut.

The ambulance came to a stop and Genesis realized that she must have closed her eyes and dozed off. Mario opened the doors and started to remove her and the stretcher.

"Mario, can we make a compromise?"

"What do you mean?"

"Since I'm sure you won't let me walk can we do a wheelchair and not the stretcher?"

"Okay. Sure. Wait here," he said and then disappeared into the hospital.

He returned with a wheelchair and helped Genesis out of the ambulance and into the chair. Mario wheeled her into the hospital and over to the desk.

The moment Genesis saw the petite Hispanic nurse behind the desk she realized where she was.

"Genesis. Are you okay?" The nurse asked.

"Hi Adrianna. Yeah, I'm fine. In fact I shouldn't even be here."

"She fell from the third floor in a building."

She turned around to see Chris standing behind her. *Where did he come from?*

"Oh dear. Do you want me to call Isis?" Adrianna asked.

"No," Genesis answered quickly. "Let's just get me checked out and out of here."

There was no way that she could let her younger sister know that she was in the ER.

"Okay, well let's get you into a room," Adrianna said. She stepped from behind the desk and over to Genesis.

"Do I have to fill anything out?"

"Nope. Isis has paperwork on file for all of you girls." Adrianna said.

Isis is Genesis' younger sister by two years. She worked at Beth Israel as a nurse in the Emergency Room. If she knew that Genesis was there she would freak out and Genesis couldn't let that happen.

Adrianna pushed Genesis through a set of automatic doors that lead to the rest of the hospital.

She sat in the exam room growing impatient by the second. Not only was Isis a nurse at the hospital but she was also due for work any minute. The last thing she needed was for Isis to show up and find her there.

Just as Genesis was working up the nerve to leave the room and demand that someone see her, the door opened. In walked one of the most beautiful black men she believed she'd ever seen. He looked like an African God.

"Hi. I'm Dr. Alex Taylor. Sorry to keep you waiting," he said and flashed his perfectly pearly whites at her.

"That's okay," she said. Her anger began melting away. She wanted to scold herself. *Why do I always turn into a little schoolgirl whenever a cute man is near?*

He looked down at the clipboard he was holding. Which she assumed was her chart.

"Well Officer Battle, I hear you took quite a fall," he sat the chart down and sat on a stool. He moved the stool so that he was sitting directly in front of her.

She suddenly wished that she were in her uniform and not the mandatory hospital gown. She felt so exposed.

Dr. Taylor began examining her, she assumed, looking for broken bones or maybe a bullet wound. She wanted to tell him he wouldn't find any but she kept her mouth shut. Every so often he asked her if she had any pain in the area he touched. She answered no every time.

"Lay back please," he said.

She scooted back on the bed and laid back. Dr. Taylor began checking her abdomen.

"Any relation to Isis Battle?"

"Yes, she's my sister."

He glanced up and looked into her eyes. She wanted to shrink under his gaze. He continued with his exam.

"I can see it now. In the eyes," he said absentmindedly.

"You're kidding me right?"

"What?" he asked "Sit up please." She did.

"My eyes are green. Isis' eyes are blue. We do not have the same eyes." She thought he was cute but clearly blind. Or maybe this was his weird way of trying to hit on her. Although they had different eye colors they shared many similarities he could have chosen from.

Genesis had green eyes while Isis' eyes were blue, Jonah's eyes were gray, Liberty's eyes were hazel and Freedom had brown eyes but they were very light and stood out against her darker complexion. They all shared a full head of thick curly hair. Not all of them wore their curls. Genesis wore her hair straight for work, Freedom currently wore her hair in braids and Liberty kept her hair straight at all times. The hair, their full lips and their wide noses were all attributes they each shared.

Dr. Taylor had his pick of ways to point out their similarities. She didn't understand why he would choose their eyes.

"Never said you guys had the same eyes," he said. He was lightly touching around her neck. "You two share a look."

"Oh." Genesis felt like a complete idiot. "Sorry."

"Don't worry about it. Believe it or not I am aware of Isis' blue eyes," he said. "I don't think there is anything seriously wrong with you. You do have some bruising around your neck here and there is a large cut on the back of your neck."

"I have bruises?" Genesis had been sure that there would be no evidence of her fight.

"Yes. I want to get you up to x-ray so that we can be certain that nothing is broken. I wouldn't want your sister to come after me."

"Okay."

The mention of her sister made her glance up at the wall clock. *7:30.*

"Is that time right?" Genesis asked, pointing to the clock..

Dr. Taylor turned to look at it.

"Yeah, it's right."

"Can we hurry all of this up?" She hadn't realized that it had gotten so late.

"Don't want to be here when your sister arrives?"

"No, I don't."

"I'll send a nurse right in," he said as he turned and left the room, taking her chart with him.

Genesis didn't have to wait long. A nurse was in her room in a matter of seconds. She stitched up her neck and than carted her up to x-ray. Once the x-rays were finished, she was put back into her room to wait for Dr. Taylor.

Genesis continued to watch the clock while she waited for the results of her x-ray. She needed to be out of the hospital before Isis showed up.

Dr. Taylor came back into the room moments later.

"Your x-rays were clear. Aside from the bruising and cut on your neck, there doesn't appear to be anything wrong with you. You are a lucky girl and you're free to leave."

He handed her papers to sign.

"Thank you." Genesis signed the papers and handed them back. He gave her a copy.

"You better hurry," he said before leaving the room. Genesis was pretty sure that he was laughing at her.

She looked up at the time. *Crap.* Genesis jumped down from the bed and began dressing.

TaQuanda Taylor

Fully dressed in her uniform, she left the exam room and made her way to the exit. Genesis spotted Isis first. She seemed to be in her own world and not paying much attention. *This may work in my favor.* Genesis was kind of glad that Isis hadn't listened when she had given her sisters the speech about being aware of their surroundings at all times.

Genesis pulled her long brown hair loose from its ponytail and let it fall over her face. It was the closest thing she had to a disguise. She had almost made it to the door when her name was called.

"Genie?"

Genesis stopped and slowly turned to face her sister.

"Hey Ice, what's going on?"

"You tell me. What are you doing here?" Isis asked. She walked over to Genesis. *Crap.*

"Oh, I just had to see a doctor." Genesis tried to inch slowly towards the door because Isis was giving her a quick once over.

"Are you hurt?"

"No, I'm fine."

"What happened to your neck?" *Double crap. This is why I was trying to get away.*

Isis rarely missed anything and Genesis knew given the time she would notice the bruising on her neck.

"I'll tell you at home." Genesis tried to drop the conversation.

"Promise?"

"Yeah, I promise. I really have to go." Genesis walked over to Chris

---

16

who was waiting by the door.

Chapter 2: Isis

Isis watched as her sister hurried out of the hospital. She couldn't believe that she had been here and worse Isis had almost missed her.

Isis loved her job and when she stepped through the automatic doors, that was what she had been thinking about. She saw Genesis' partner Chris standing by the door when she had entered. His presence hadn't fully registered at first. It wasn't until she was almost at the admissions desk when it hit her.

Isis spun around to ask him where Genesis was and then she saw her. Genesis had actually tried sneaking out. Like putting her hair in her face was going to make it hard to recognize her.

Isis knew that Genesis was probably trying to avoid explaining her presence but it didn't matter. She had to know why her sister was in the emergency room.

Although Isis loved her job, the thought that one of her sisters needed emergency medical care made her stomach hurt. For now she would let Genesis leave but would hold her to her promise and find out what happened once she got home or find out from someone working.

"Hey Isis."

She turned around to face Adrianna who was sitting behind the admission desk.

"Hey girl," Isis said. "Do you know why my sister was here?"

"Something happened at work and if you want to know more ask her," Adrianna answered.

When it came to Adrianna's job she was very serious about it. Most doctors and nurses gossiped about different patients but Adrianna was squeaky clean in that department. She took patient confidentiality very seriously.

"I wouldn't dare have you tell me anything you weren't comfortable sharing." Isis knew she wouldn't get anywhere with her. "Who saw her?"

"Dr. Taylor and if he knows what is good for him he wouldn't say anything either," Adrianna said.

"What do you mean?"

"I mean if you want to know what is up with *your* sister than you should ask *your* sister," Adrianna responded.

"Got it," Isis said.

Isis figured she would just get the truth out of Dr. Taylor. She walked through the automatic doors and straight to the locker room to change.

Isis dressed in a pair of clean scrubs, pulled her hair back into a ponytail and left the locker room. Her first mission was to find Dr. Taylor. She needed to know what happened to Genesis and she couldn't wait until she got home later. She walked over to the nurse's station.

"Hey Lee." Isis greeted the cute and very gay male nurse sitting in front of one of the computers.

"Oh good, you're here. Dr. Taylor is in room 2," he said.

"How did you know I was looking for him?"

"I didn't. He said for you to meet him when you got in."

"Oh. Thanks."

Maybe Dr. Taylor knew how worried Isis would be and had already planned to tell her what had happened.

She raised her hand to knock on the door before entering and instead pressed her hand on the door to steady herself. She was feeling a little dizzy. The dizzy spell passed and she knocked on the door and then opened it.

"I'm sorry, I didn't mean to interrupt."

Dr. Taylor was seeing a patient.

"You're not interrupting. You are right on time." Dr. Taylor said. He glanced over his shoulder and smiled at her.

Dr. Taylor was a beautiful man. The nurse's had taken to calling him Dr. McDreamy. Not because he favored Patrick Dempsey but because Grey's Anatomy made it acceptable to lust after handsome doctors. If there were going to be a McDreamy in this hospital it would be Dr. Taylor.

"Can I help with anything?" Isis asked.

"Yes. You can help me explain to Mrs. Carter that she is going to be just fine," he said.

Mrs. Carter was clutching her chest in pain and moaning in agony. She certainly didn't look okay. Isis looked at Dr. Taylor questioning him silently. He mouthed 'gas' to her. Isis nodded in understanding. Dr. Taylor checked Mrs. Carter out and she was merely experiencing

TaQuanda Taylor
gas pains.

Dr. Taylor picked up her chart and began writing.

"Mrs. Carter, the pain that you are feeling is from gas. It will subside," Isis said reassuringly.

"How do you know? You just got here," Mrs. Carter groaned.

"Ma'am what you have is gas. Now I can give you something to help make you feel a little more comfortable but the pain will pass," Dr. Taylor said.

"I want a different doctor," she managed to say.

"Okay." Dr. Taylor didn't seem fazed by the request at all.

Isis followed him out of the room.

"Get her something for the gas," he said and handed her the chart. He was going to ignore her request for a different doctor.

"Okay. You saw my sister today." Isis said.

"Yes I did."

"Well?"

"Well what?"

"What happened?"

"I can't discuss that with you."

"You discuss patients with me all the time."

"Not when that patient is your family," he said. "Look, I'll tell you this and only this." He placed his hand on her arm. "Your sister is fine."

"Really? That's it?"

"Really," he laughed. "Don't worry. Your sister is one tough chick."

"Yeah. I know."

"I really want to kiss you right now," he said. He was leaning really close to her now.

"If you did, someone would see us."

"Then I'll wait until we're alone. Don't worry about your sister." He turned and walked away.

Easy for him to say. Isis knew she shouldn't worry but she couldn't help herself and she didn't think she should be the only one. Before Isis took care of Mrs. Carter and her gas, she needed to make a phone call.

Isis took her phone out of the pocket on her scrubs and hit one of the speed dials. Jonah answered after a couple of rings.

"What's up?"

"Genesis was in the ER."

"What?" Jonah's voice raised a few octaves. Isis knew her sister would join in on the worrying.

"She was leaving as I was coming in."

"Did you find out what happened? Is she okay?"

"She said she would tell me when I got home tonight."

"I'm going to call her."

TaQuanda Taylor

"Okay. Bye."

"Bye."

They disconnected the call.

Isis walked back into Mrs. Carter's room with what Dr. Taylor suggested. The air got knocked out of her. There was such a foul smell in the room. Mrs. Carter must have relieved her gas.

She was out of her hospital gown and dressed in her clothes.

"I feel much better dear. I guess you two were right," she said.

Isis was too afraid to speak, so she just nodded. She wished she had a mask or a giant can of air freshener. One person should not be able to make that much stink.

"I'll get your discharge papers." Isis tried not to breath in the smell.

"Okay," Mrs. Carter said. She opened her mouth and let lose the foulest burp, which was followed by an even fouler fart.

Isis hurried from the room as fast as she could and gasped for clean air the moment the door was closed. *Why couldn't she have waited until she was home before she had done that.*

Isis walked to the nurse's station and found Adrianna at one of the computers. She took a seat at the next computer.

"You're still here?" Isis asked.

"Yeah. I have to take care of a few things and then I am out of here," she answered.

"Do you want to do me a favor?"

"Depends on the favor."

"I was wondering if you could discharge a patient for me."

"What's wrong with the patient?"

"Nothing," Isis lied. Adrianna stopped what she was doing and looked at her. "Alright, gas."

"Must be some bad gas."

"You have no idea."

"I'll do it for you. If you tell me what is up with you and McDreamy."

Adrianna wasn't a fan of gossiping about patients but when it came to other's personal lives she was all in. You could usually find her at the center of most of that gossip.

"I don't know what you are talking about." Isis turned to the computer and began printing Mrs. Carter's discharge papers.

"Nurse Lee said he saw the two of you and you were looking awfully close. So spill," she said.

"There's nothing to spill. You know what? I can handle the discharge." Sometimes you had to pick your battles and this was one battle she didn't want to have.

Isis stood, retrieved the papers from the printer and left the area. She could hear Adrianna snicker behind her. They were best friends and Isis would have loved to tell her every juicy detail, but she and Dr. Taylor had agreed to keep things quiet.

Isis braced herself as she walked into Mrs. Carter's room. If it were possible the smell had worsened.

"I have your discharge papers. I just need you to sign and then you are free to go," Isis choked out.

"Okay. Thank you. I need to get home and eat something. I feel so empty," she said.

Isis held her lips together to keep from laughing. She could only imagine why Mrs. Carter felt empty. She took the signed papers and left the room.

Dr. Taylor headed in Isis' direction. She started thinking of ways to trick him into the room. He had pulled her onto the case and it was only right that he suffered as well.

"Hey."

"Hey." Dr. Taylor said as he continued past her. She felt a little hurt by the rejection. They weren't all over each other in public but she did expect him to at least acknowledge her.

He walked down the corridor and approached a woman. She was beautiful, like a movie star. She smiled up at him and touched him lightly on the arm. The touch was very familiar to the touch he had given Isis earlier.

Isis wasn't a jealous person but she felt signs of jealousy when she saw him with that woman. There was also a bit of worry mixed in there.

Dr. Taylor placed his hand on the small of the woman's back and led her down the corridor. Isis didn't want to but she couldn't help herself. She followed them.

They seemed very familiar with each other and that made her feel uneasy.

They ducked into the stairwell and Isis walked over to the door. She stepped closer to look inside and heard a noise from behind her.

Trying not to look suspicious, Isis moved from the door and turned to face whoever was approaching.

An orderly pushed a patient by on a gurney. He nodded at her and she smiled in return. Isis hoped she didn't look as guilty as she felt.

The orderly continued past and Isis started to move but another wave of dizziness hit her. She pressed her back against the wall and took a deep breath. The dizzy spell passed. *I hope I'm not coming down with anything.* Isis went back to the door and peered inside.

They were gone. *Where did they go?*

Isis opened the door and stepped into the stairwell. She was about to go up when she heard voices coming from below. She shouldn't be here. She should be minding her own business but curiosity was killing her. She had to know who the woman was.

Isis stepped up to the railing and peered over. They looked like they were in a heated discussion.

"Maybe you should stop ignoring me." The woman was saying.

Dr. Taylor stepped away from the woman. Isis couldn't see him. She grabbed the rail and leaned forward. The papers slipped from her hand. *Oh crap.*

"Who's there?" Dr. Taylor yelled up.

Isis ran to the door to leave but it wouldn't open. She could hear Dr. Taylor ascending the stairs. *Please let me be anywhere but here.*

Dr. Taylor was going to catch her snooping and that wouldn't be good. Isis knew that she shouldn't have followed him. *Why isn't this door opening?*

Isis could hear him getting closer. She closed her eyes and sent up a silent prayer to God, to please get her out of this stairwell. Another dizzy spell came over her. She leaned forward to steady herself. Isis closed her eyes pressed her hand on the door. It felt weird.

The texture she felt against her hand was familiar but she knew that it wasn't the door. She opened her eyes and took a quick intake of breath.

Her hand was pressed firmly against a locker door, her locker door to be exact. Isis moved her hand and stood upright. She looked slowly around the locker room.

How did I get here? The last thing Isis remembered was being on the stairs and praying that Dr. Taylor wouldn't find her. She had felt a little sick but then that was it. She didn't remember leaving the stairs or walking to the locker room.

This doesn't make any sense.

Isis could hear someone turning the knob on the door. That small noise spooked her. She felt like she was about to be caught doing something she shouldn't be doing. Isis practically jumped out of her skin.

Isis stood in the middle of the floor and looked around. She was in one of the women's bathrooms. If she had to guess it was the one near the nurse's station.

How did I get here? Something wasn't right. She had just been in the locker room and now she was in the bathroom. She couldn't have just appeared here. That was impossible. There had to be a rational, scientific, maybe even medical reason for this.

Medical. Of course. *Why didn't I think of that before?* She hadn't been feeling well before. She must have experienced a blackout. She just couldn't think of what could be so wrong with her that she was blacking out. She had to sit down.

Isis walked into one of the stalls and sat down on the seat. The door opened and frightened her. She threw her arms out and held the walls of the stall to keep herself steady.

Isis felt like she might faint.

Adrianna passed the stalls but backed up and stared at her.

"Are you okay?" she asked.

"No. I'm not really feeling so good."

"Why don't you go home? I can cover the rest of your shift."

"Are you sure? You've been here all night."

"I'm sure. Besides, you look like crap and I'll be getting paid."

Isis tried to manage a laugh but failed.

"Thanks."

"Don't worry about it. Feel better." Adrianna walked away and entered one of the empty stalls.

Isis needed to get out of there and into her bed. She stood and exited the stall, because she couldn't remember what happened in the bathroom, she washed her hands.

Isis stepped out of the bathroom and nearly ran right into Dr. Taylor. This was not what she needed right now. She didn't remember what happened but if he had caught her, she wasn't ready to talk about it.

"Hey. You don't look so good. Are you okay?"

"I've been better. I was actually going to go home."

"Okay," he looked nervous. "Do you want me to take a look at you?"

"No, I think I just need to lay down."

He hesitated for a moment like there was more that he wanted to say.

"Mrs. Carter get out today?"

"Huh?" The question confused her for a second. "Yeah. Sorry I didn't page you. You had already signed off on it."

"It's okay. I found her discharge papers," he said. He held the papers up so that Isis could see them. *Oh no.* If she hadn't been caught, those papers were all the evidence he needed.

"I can take those." Isis reached for the papers. She didn't want to look at him but she knew that she couldn't avoid his eyes forever. He moved the papers away.

"It's cool. I'll put them in her chart, you get out of here." He didn't address the fact that he had found the papers in the stairs.

Isis was almost positive that she saw guilt in his eyes. The thought that he was feeling guilty about something made her stomach twist into a knot. She had to get home.

Isis made it to the locker room and changed into her street clothes. Her hands were shaking. She took a seat on the bench to steady herself. *What is wrong with me? Why am I getting so worked up?* She had never been this way over a boy before. Isis wasn't that type of girl. You know, the super clingy, he's-gonna-be-my-husband, type. That girl just wasn't Isis.

Isis was the, let's-hangout-and-see-where-it-goes, type. It usually never went anywhere and she had always been cool with that.

At an early age Isis had learned that men were not dependable. Her mom had five daughters and not one dad was present. Men came and went. She grew to enjoy the first and not dwell on the second.

This was different. Isis had followed him because she was jealous. That only meant one thing. She was falling for Dr. Taylor.

When had this happened? Why didn't I stop it from happening? Falling for a man only led to two things, a child and heartbreak and Isis had no use for either.

Isis suddenly had this urge to go to him. She wanted to tell him that it had been her in the stairs. That she didn't want to hide anymore, that she was ready to tell people about them. But there was a part of her that wouldn't let her go.

It was like the two parts were fighting each other. She knew physically that she was still in the locker room but she was sure that she was staring directly at Dr. Taylor. He was standing at the nurse's station.

That was impossible. She couldn't be in the locker room and near Dr. Taylor.

Isis needed to pull herself together. She closed her eyes and took two deep breaths. She opened them again and all that was in front of her was her open locker. She needed to get out of there.

Isis stood, closed the locker and left the locker room.

She walked towards the exit and stopped in her tracks. It was like an invisible wall had formed in front of her. Standing not far from the exit was the woman Dr. Taylor had been with. This day was just getting better and better. She didn't know why she was standing there staring at her.

There was no way that the woman could know who Isis was. Isis started towards the exit and the woman turned around.

It was almost like she knew exactly who Isis was. She looked directly into Isis' eyes. Out of pure instinct her pace slowed.

Did the woman want to say something to her? Did Isis want to say something to the woman?

Before Isis could pull her big girl panties on and approach this woman, she hurried from the hospital. Now was not the time to begin fighting over a man. Isis had made it this far having never stooped so low and she wasn't about to begin now.

JONAH

Jonah stopped at the door and let a shudder run over her. Once that feeling was gone, she carried a box of liquor behind the bar.

"Jo, are you okay?"

Jonah turned and faced her co-worker Danielle. Danielle was a petite blond who worked behind the bar with her. Jonah had recently moved up from a Hooters waitress to bartender.

The job wasn't as bad as everyone thought it was. The tips were good and the guys didn't try to fill you up as much as people believed. Every so often you may get a drunk who got a little too hands-on but it was always dealt with.

"Yeah. I just keep getting this weird creepy crawly feeling."

"You mean like a cold chill?"

"No. It's more like a million bugs are crawling over my skin."

"Ew. Okay, now you just made my skin crawl," Danielle said as she shuddered.

"Sorry," Jonah laughed and shuddered again. "That is the third one in the last fifteen minutes."

"Really?"

"Yeah. The first one happened a little after five this morning. It woke me up. They just keep happening."

"Do you think something is wrong?"

When Jonah thought about her question it did kind of feel like a warning. Maybe she was just worried about Isis' call.

"You know what? I'm probably just worried about Genesis," Jonah spoke her earlier thought.

"Still haven't reached her?"

"Nope. I think she might be ignoring me on purpose."

A shaggy haired man walked over to the bar and sat.

"It's a little early to be drinking, don't you think?" Jonah asked him.

"It's five o'clock somewhere," he answered.

"What will it be, Ernie?" Jonah asked.

"Bud Light."

Jonah took a glass and filled it with the beer. She placed it in front of him.

"What some food to go with that?"

"No, I'm fine."

"Well, let me know if you change your mind." Jonah turned to Danielle who was unpacking the liquor. "I'm going to go try Genesis again."

TaQuanda Taylor
"Okay, take your time," she said.

Jonah walked from behind the bar and entered the back room. She took her phone out from where it was tucked into her shorts and pressed one of her speed dials.

The phone rang twice and then Genesis' voicemail came on.

"This is Officer Genesis Battle. Sorry that I have missed your call. Please leave a detailed message and I will call you right back." BEEP.

Jonah had already left her two messages and she didn't want to be an annoyance. Which is why she tried to make this message shorter than the first two.

"Genie, it's Jo. Call me back ASAP or I will come find you."

She hung up the phone and stared at it. That should get her attention.

Genesis should be home by now and Jonah knew she wasn't sleeping. She didn't fall asleep immediately. So why wasn't she answering her phone?

She sighed and went back to work. She would find out whatever it was that she was trying to keep to herself.

No secrets. That was the rule. Genesis couldn't keep anything to herself. Not even if she really wanted to.

She would just have to stop obsessing over this and hopefully whatever was ailing her would go away.

Chapter 3: Genesis

Genesis walked into Lieutenant Jonathan Prado's office. She could feel everyone's eyes on her. They had all been staring from the moment she had arrived back from the hospital. Genesis was already nervous and the stares were not making it any easier. If Chris had been with her it would be a little easier but he said he had things to do.

"Close the door and have a seat," Lieutenant Prado said.

Jonathan Prado was a handsome man. It was like God himself had hand sculpted him. He was of Cuban decent and had retained his accent even after twenty years in the US. He was the type of man that women tended to lose the ability to speak around. Which was why she was nervous about being asked into his office.

Genesis followed instructions and closed the door and then took a seat across from his desk.

"You look well," he said.

Brown eyes locked with hers. She was finding it very hard to sit still. She hoped that he couldn't see her blush.

"Yeah. I'm fine. I told Chris that I didn't need to go to the emergency room." Wow. She couldn't believe that she had managed to get that out. Her mouth was extremely dry.

"From what I heard of today's events, Chris was right in making sure that you got checked out," he said.

Genesis tried to swallow around the lump in her throat. "Well, the doctor said I'm okay."

"Yes. I can see that." He seemed to look right through her. "We can't say the same thing about Mr. Washburn." He looked down at his desk.

For a split second she had forgotten all about Mark Washburn. Lieutenant Prado picked up a piece of paper from his desk. "Mr. Washburn has a broken jaw along with several other bruises and scratches conclusive with being in a fight. He has two broken ribs and a fractured tibia which seems to be a result of the fall you two took." He put down the paper and looked at her.

"Damn." *Did I really just say that?*

"Damn indeed, considering your lack of injuries." His eyes bore into her.

"I have injuries," Genesis blurted before she realized it. For some reason today she was having a hard time keeping her mouth shut. He didn't say anything just stared at her. So she continued. "I have a cut on the back of my neck from the fall and these bruises from when he was choking me." Her injuries did not compare to Washburn's but she felt this urge to let him know that she hadn't walked away completely unharmed. Maybe it was because she was feeling a little like a freak due to the lack of injuries.

Genesis' hair was back in its standard ponytail so her neck was pretty visible.

He finally looked away and opened a drawer in the desk. He removed a small digital camera. He stood and crossed the room until he was standing in front of her.

"Don't move." *Okay.* He aimed the camera at her and took three pictures. She felt weird with him snapping photos of her, mainly because she wanted to take the camera and snap photos of him. He should be in a magazine not in a police station. Genesis tried to stop her wayward thoughts.

He then moved behind her. He took the tail end of her ponytail and moved it so that it was hanging over her shoulder. She could feel his fingers touch her neck as he removed the bandage. She hoped he didn't feel the involuntary shudder that ran through her body. He didn't seem to notice.

The bandage was gone and her wound was exposed. He took two photos. "Stay still." He walked back over to his desk. He put the camera back into its drawer and then turned his back to her. When he turned back around she noticed that he had a first aid kit in his hands.

He crossed back over to Genesis and gently re-bandaged her wound.

Wound safely secured under a new bandage, he took his seat.

"I'm giving you a couple of days off." Lieutenant Prado said.

"Excuse me," Genesis asked. She was really hoping that she didn't hear him right. "I'm fine I don't need any time off."

"I think you do and so does the Commissioner," he said.

"Wait a minute. Am I being suspended?" He didn't need to answer the question because she already knew the answer. "Why? I didn't do anything wrong."

"You ignored an order from your superior and chased after a man when your police cruiser was within distance. The man has suffered injuries that requires him to remain in the hospital while you have suffered a scratch."

TaQuanda Taylor

Unbelievable. They were punishing her because she *wasn't* hurt on the job. What sense did that make? She felt herself getting angry.

"So because I didn't break like he did I'm getting punished?" She couldn't help but voice her thoughts aloud.

"I'm sure if you take a second to calm down you can see the bigger picture here," he said. His face gave nothing more away.

After a second what he was trying to say sunk in.

"He's trying to say that I used excessive force?" As she said the words she knew that was exactly the case.

The Commissioner had really been cracking down on police brutality claims. It was a touchy subject.

"Right now he's not saying anything. He hasn't woken up." Lieutenant Prado said calmly.

"But you guys want to come out a head of this in case he does."

"I hope you understand," he said.

She was mad, really mad but she understood. "So how long am I suspended?"

"We will talk again on Monday and take it from there."

There was nothing more to say. Because something weird was going on with her, she was being suspended from her job. A job she didn't even want in the beginning. She stood to leave but he stopped her before she could get out.

"I'm going to need your badge and gun." *Unbelievable.*

Genesis removed her badge and gun and placed them on his desk. She couldn't believe that this was happening to her. She didn't want to stay in this office a moment longer so she found her escape.

Nothing had changed since she first stepped into Lieutenant Prado's office. Everyone was once again staring at her. After everything that had just happened she was not in the mood. She walked as calmly as she could muster through the station.

She just needed to get to the locker room and then out of there.

She felt the threat of tears starting to build. What will she do if she completely lost this job?

It wasn't the dream. Being a lawyer was the dream but at the moment that wasn't a possibility. This job paid well and it allowed her to do what she needed to do to take care of her sisters. If she didn't have this job what was she left with? Retail? Restaurants?

There was nothing wrong with working in restaurants. Hell. Jonah worked in a restaurant. It was just that she thought it would be taking a step back if she did.

"Are you okay?" Genesis nearly jumped out of her skin at the voice.

She turned around and found Officer Tina Greene at her locker. She hadn't heard anyone enter.

"Yeah. I'm fine." Genesis turned back around and finished changing.

"I heard about what happened."

"What are you talking about?" She didn't mean to but her voice rose a few octaves.

"The whole thing that happened with the guy you tried to arrest," she said innocently.

"You don't know what you're talking about. First, I didn't try to arrest him, I did." Genesis didn't know why she felt the need to clarify things but the fact that people were gossiping about her was really pissing her off. "Second, you might want to try minding your own business."

Tina jumped at the infliction in Genesis' voice. She turned back to her own locker.

She didn't deserve Genesis' wrath but she was the only one in the room.

Genesis stormed out of the locker room fully dressed in street clothes and ran into a solid form. She looked up and stared into Chris' face. This was the person she was mad at.

"Hey. Are you okay?" he asked.

"Yeah, no thanks to you."

"What?"

"Did you know?"

He looked away. When he looked back he looked sorry. "Yeah."

"How could you?" She was so mad at him. She felt like he had stabbed her in the back.

"I didn't do anything but my job. If you had listened to me we wouldn't be having this conversation."

"You're supposed to be my friend."

"I'm your superior."

"You never have to worry about me making that mistake again." She stormed past him.

___

She knew that she was acting like a child but she was so mad. She couldn't blame it on him but for right now she would. It was the only way she knew how to channel her anger. She had never been this upset before.

As she walked away from Chris she noticed that everyone was still staring at her. She wanted to go off on them but she knew that causing a scene would probably not be the best thing to do. At least there was still some part of her brain that was thinking rationally.

She pushed open the glass door that lead to the outside world and it shattered. She looked down at the shards of broken glass and up at the frame. It was hanging from the hinges. *Did I do that?* She looked behind her and everyone was watching.

So much for getting them to stop staring at me.

"Are you okay?" Chris was standing beside her.

"Yeah."

"I'll get someone to clean this up. It was probably loose," he said. He didn't seem to think that she had broken the door.

She didn't know what else to say so she just turned and left.

ISIS

Isis stepped into the apartment and let out a sigh of relief. She was starting to feel better and more like herself. She didn't know what happened while she was at work but she was happy to be home where she felt safe.

"Who is that?" Genesis called from the living room.

TaQuanda Taylor

She had expected Genesis to be asleep but she was happy that she was awake because she needed to talk to her. She then suddenly remembered that Genesis had been at the hospital, which meant something had happened.

She walked the few short steps it took and into the living room. Genesis was standing in front of the couch. She had changed out of her uniform and was dressed in shorts and a t-shirt.

"What are you doing home?" Genesis asked.

"I wasn't feeling good. Hey, what happened today?" she asked. She walked over to stand in front of Genesis.

Genesis didn't seem to hear her question. "What? Are you okay?" she asked. She pressed the back of her hand to Isis' forehead. "You don't feel warm."

"I feel better now," she said.

"Well what was wrong?" Genesis instinctively jumped into the big sister/mother role that she had perfected over the years.

"I was feeling dizzy and I was forgetting things. Actually I still don't remember everything that happened while I was at the hospital." Her earlier concerns about Genesis' presence in the hospital were momentarily forgotten. Like her, Isis jumped into a familiar role. The little-sister-take-care-of-me role. Letting Genesis take care of her was nothing new. It was what she was good at.

"What? Did you let somebody check you out?" Genesis ushered Isis to sit down and sat beside her.

"No, I didn't let anybody check me out. I'm fine."

"If you're so fine why did you leave work?"

"Because when I was there I wasn't feeling well." Isis remembered that Genesis had been in the hospital. "It's probably because I was so focused on trying to figure out why you were there." Isis tried to turn the conversation around.

Isis watched as Genesis' expression changed. She got her. Time to get back to her original concern. Besides, that could be why she hadn't been feeling well.

"What happened to you today? Why were you in the hospital?"

Genesis hesitated. "No secrets, remember?" Isis tried to urge her on.

"I chased a perp today and we kind of fell over a banister from the third floor." Genesis said.

Isis was not expecting that. "What? Kind of fell? How do you kind of fall? OHMYGOD! Are you okay? Did you break anything? Why aren't you still in the hospital? Why would they let you go?" Isis was hurling questions at Genesis at lighting speed.

Isis couldn't believe that Genesis fell over a banister.

"I'm fine." Genesis tried to stop her stampede of questions. "I did get a nasty gash on the back of my neck."

Isis slowly moved to look at the back of her neck. She didn't want to hurt Genesis if she was in any pain. She was grateful to see the bandage on Genesis' neck, happy that she hadn't removed it.

Genesis had always been the protector, even when they were really young. No matter what she always tried to be the strong one. She would brag about the fact that she never got sick or hurt. So hearing about what had happened to her made Isis want to cry.

"I'll change the bandage later." Isis tried to calm herself down because she didn't want to upset Genesis.

———

TaQuanda Taylor

"Okay," she said.

"What about these bruises on your neck?"

Isis frowned at the bruises on Genesis' neck. They were as defined as they were when she saw them in the hospital. The thing was, it looked like they were fading. Isis blinked, trying to clear her eyes.

"The guy was choking me right before we fell." Genesis said calmly, almost a little too calmly.

"Really? Does it hurt?" Isis looked back at the bruises. What she saw was impossible. The marks were almost completely invisible.

"Yeah. He's actually still in the hospital."

"Oh." Isis stopped herself from saying 'good'. She knew it was insensitive. "Did you break anything?"

"No. Nothing's broken." Isis let out a sigh of relief. " That's not all." Genesis looked like she wasn't sure if she should keep talking. Isis was not sure it could get worse.

"What is it?" Isis probed.

"Um, I sort of got shot. Like four times." Genesis said slowly making sure Isis heard every word.

Chapter 4: Genesis

Once the words were out she wished she had never said them. They had a no secrets promise between them but the look on Isis' face made her wish she had broken that promise. She stopped herself from reaching over and tapping Isis' chin so that she would close her mouth. Isis would need some time.

Genesis tried to give Isis the time she needed so they just sat and stared at each other. Isis' mouth was still hanging open.

Genesis couldn't take the silence anymore. "Ice?"

Isis closed her mouth and took a deep breath. "Shot?"

The word came out as a barely audible whisper.

"Yeah."

She could tell that Isis was trying to compose herself. "So what, the bullets grazed you?"

Genesis knew Isis would want more information. *Here goes nothing.*

"No. The bullets didn't graze me, they penetrated skin."

"What?" Isis' face dropped.

"Isis please don't freak out." Genesis said in an attempt to calm her.

"Okay," she said. She looked like she was on the verge of crying.

The only way to solve this was to give Isis some proof that she was okay. She just wasn't sure how Isis was going to react.

Genesis lifted her right arm and pointed to the middle of her bicep. She knew what Isis would see. Nothing. "This is where one of the bullets went in." Genesis remembered where she was hit because she had felt it, although it hadn't hurt.

Isis stared at her arm. Confused blue eyes meet nervous green ones. *Might as well continue.*

Genesis lifted her left arm, rolled her sleeve up and pointed to just below her shoulder. "This is where another bullet when it."

Isis looked at both spots. Genesis kept going. She pulled down the collar of her shirt and pointed out the shot that probably should have killed her. "Also here."

Isis eyes moved to that spot. Genesis pointed to her right thigh. "And here."

Isis looked at all four spots and then back at Genesis. Genesis braced herself for the next response.

"I don't understand," she finally said.

"Me neither."

"You were shot?"

"Yeah."

"But?" Isis raised her hand and touched the spot on Genesis right arm where she was shot.

"No wounds." Genesis finished her thought.

"What are you saying?"

"That I got shot but I don't have any wounds."

"How?" Isis asked tentatively.

"I don't know." This whole thing was new to Genesis. Nothing like this had ever happened before. Sure she avoided sickness but this was not the same. She should be in a hospital room hooked up to machines. The bullet that entered near her collar should have done a lot of damage. She should also be completely covered in bruises.

The fall that Genesis had taken left the other guy in the hospital. Not to mention the number of times her face had taken a blow from him. There wasn't so much as a scratch on her face. The only evidence she had to prove that she had been in an altercation was the bruising around her neck and the cut. Genesis already knew before Isis saw her neck that the bruises were fading. She had looked in the mirror when she got home.

Isis didn't say anything for a while. Genesis didn't want to push her so she sat back and waited patiently. She knew this was a lot to take in. She was still trying to take it all in herself.

The silence was very ominous. Genesis wished she knew what Isis was thinking.

"Let me know when we're good cause I'm not done," Genesis said.

"Oh God! There's more?" She didn't look like she could take another bombshell.

"Just a little one," Genesis said trying to reassure her.

"Oh thank God for the small things." Isis said sarcastically.

"I think I broke a door today." Genesis spit out.

"What?"

"Yeah. I was kind of mad and the next thing I knew the door was in pieces. Literally. There was glass everywhere."

"Okay, so, just one question. What are you?"

"What?" Genesis couldn't believe Isis had just asked her that. What was worse was that she was completely serious.

"You say you got shot but you have no bullet wounds. You claim that you used super strength and broke a door. Those bruises around your neck are gone."

Before Genesis had time to react Isis stood, reached behind her and removed the bandage.

"There's nothing back there." She held up the bandage. "This was covering nothing. So what are you?"

"What do you mean what am I? I'm your sister."

"Are you sure?"

"Seriously?"

"Are you like my sister who was bit by a genetically altered spider? Or did you die and get licked by magical cats?"

Genesis couldn't stop the laughter that spilled out. "I'm not Spiderman or Cat Woman. I'm me."

Isis looked at her suspiciously. "Okay."

"Okay?" Genesis asked. She was surprised Isis was calm.

———

"Yeah. I need a drink." She got up and left the living room. Now that was the reaction Genesis was expecting.

JONAH

Jonah's head was still messed up after Isis' call. Isis would have never called if she hadn't thought that it was something worth worrying about and now she still couldn't get Genesis on the phone.

It was pretty slow and Jonah had to keep busy. Although most of her time was spent behind the bar she still liked to help out the wait staff from time to time. She walked over to a table to clear up all of the dirty dishes. Jonah clutched the table to remain upright as a very intense chill overtook her body. She had been having them all day but they haven't been this bad.

Jonah went back to cleaning up the dishes. Her life was so different than what she thought it would be. She managed to complete one semester in college majoring in sociology. But that had to be put on hold.

Genesis had given up her dream of becoming a lawyer to take care of the sisters. She had watched her struggle to pay the bills and put Isis and her through college. Getting this job at Hooters was just supposed to help with some of the struggle.

She was bringing home pretty good money from her tips but it became harder and harder to balance school and work. The only thing she could think to do was to drop out of school.

Of course Genesis had been mad at her but she had been grateful for the help. Genesis had made a sacrifice so she had to be strong enough to make one too. Maybe once everything calmed down she could go back or maybe send Genesis to school.

Jonah carried the bin of dirty dishes to the back. Another chill ran up her spine. These chills were giving her a really sick feeling. She set the bin down because her hands were shaking.

She took a couple of deep breaths and told herself that Genesis was fine. She was worried about her but if there was something serious going on she was sure she would tell her. They didn't have secrets with each other. Jonah would just have to put this out of her head until she got home.

Putting the eerie feeling out of her mind, she went back to helping with the customers.

ISIS

Isis walked over to the fridge and removed a Seagram's Escapes. She should be more freaked out then she was. Her sister did just tell her that she couldn't get hurt. Well, she didn't actually say that but what else would you call it?

She had no bruises or wounds and the two that she did have were gone. Isis wasn't even sure if Genesis actually did have a cut on her neck.

If she hadn't witnessed the disappearing act the marks on her neck played she might have thought Genesis was playing a nasty trick on her. It wasn't even April Fools Day.

Isis opened the Seagram's and took a long drink. That's it. That's why she was not running from the apartment screaming. She had watched it happen.

At first Isis had thought her eyes were playing tricks on her. How could her marks just disappear? But the more Genesis had talked and when Isis saw that she didn't have any wounds from getting shot Isis knew that her eyes weren't playing tricks on her.

It happened. It actually happened. What was happening she had no idea but whatever it was she was now a witness to it, or at least some of it.

Isis heard Genesis enter the kitchen before she spoke.

"Can I get one of those?"

Isis took out another Seagram's and turned to her. Isis knew she was taking a risk in getting the floor dirty but she couldn't stop herself. Isis had to see what else Genesis could do.

Instead of just closing the short distance between them and handing the bottle to her, Isis tossed it at her. Isis' throwing skills could use some work, which was why she wasn't surprised when the bottle nearly flew over Genesis' head.

Yet, to Isis' utter surprise Genesis caught it. Her hand shot up and caught the bottle before it could go any further. Isis' mouth dropped open. By all accounts she shouldn't have been able to catch it.

"What did you do that for?" she asked.

Isis pulled herself together and closed her gapping mouth.

"I wanted to see if you could catch it," Isis said.

"Because?"

"I don't know."

"Are you freaking out?" she asked wearily.

"No ... no ... not freaking out." Isis stammered.

"It's okay if you are. I'm still kind of freaking out."

TaQuanda Taylor

"What's there to freak out about? My sister is a super human." Isis said.

"Look, I'm not a super human," she said. She took a step towards Isis who took an involuntary step back.

The look on Genesis' face broke Isis' heart. She looked like Isis had just slapped her.

"I'm sorry." Isis moved towards her and this time Genesis stepped back.

"No, it's cool."

"Genesis, I'm sorry. I don't know why I did that."

"Are you afraid of me?" She looked so hurt. Isis didn't know how to answer her.

"Look, I'm going to go lay down." She turned out of the kitchen to her left and into her room. The door slammed shut, hard. The apartment shook.

"Don't be scared, I pushed it harder than I thought," she called from the room.

Isis felt utterly like crap. She didn't mean to make Genesis think that she was scared of her. Isis didn't even mean to step away from her it just sort of happened.

Now Isis had gone ahead and hurt her sister's feelings. Genesis would understand that Isis didn't mean anything by it.

Isis didn't think that Genesis was a monster. Yeah there was something weird going on but didn't the fact that she didn't run screaming from the apartment mean anything?

Who was she kidding? If the roles had been reversed and Genesis had stepped away from her like that she probably would have started crying right there. The feeling that someone was either repulsed by or scared of you was not a feeling that anyone should have. And here she was making her own sister feel that.

Isis was going to let Genesis sleep because she had had a pretty eventful day and Isis needed some air.

Isis guzzled down the rest of her drink and grabbed another from the fridge. She stepped to the window and opened it.

Isis stepped out on the fire escape and made her way up. She stepped onto the roof and walked towards the middle to sit down. She let out a sigh.

Isis was thinking that she had really screwed up. She was hoping that with some time that Genesis would forgive her and understand. It wasn't everyday that your sister dropped the kind of bombs she did.

Chapter 5: Freedom

September 5, 2014
6:30 AM

"*Hey*, time to get up." Isis said.

Freedom mumbled something unintelligible, but she was hoping that Isis understood it as "go away". She knew neither response would actually make Isis go away. As she expected, the light in the room was flicked on.

"Get up," Isis said. "Where is Liberty?"

Freedom peeked from under the covers at the empty bed across the room.

"Check Jo's room," she said.

"Alright. Get up. There are four women in this apartment that have to get ready and get out. So why don't you start," said Isis.

Freedom mouthed the words along with her. Isis said the same thing every morning when she tried to get Freedom awake for school.

The room got quiet. Isis must have left to wake Jonah and Liberty and in doing so she left the light on. Freedom tried to burrow her head under her covers but it did nothing. The light was too bright.

I wish the light would turn off. The light went out and Freedom was once again in darkness.

55

"Thanks Libby," Freedom said. She was sure that her sister had turned the light off.

There was no response. Freedom moved the covers and looked around the room. She was alone.

Maybe Liberty turned the light off and then left the room. She didn't believe that. She hadn't heard Liberty come into the room.

Freedom sat up and looked around the empty room. As much as she didn't want to be, she was fully awake now. *Might as well start getting ready for school.*

She climbed out of the bed and moved to turn the light back on. Before she could touch the switch it moved to the ON position and the light came on.

She took a step back and stared at the switch. Freedom reached out for the switch again and it moved to the OFF position. She was standing in her dark room staring at the switch. Her arm still outstretched towards it.

Freedom didn't know how long she had been standing in that one spot when Liberty entered.

"What? Did you forget how to turn the light on?" Liberty joked. She flipped the switch and the light turned on.

Liberty moved over to her side of the room and began rummaging through her dresser.

"What are you doing?" Liberty asked.

Freedom turned around. Liberty was standing next to her, staring.

"Nothing."

"Okay. I call dibs on the shower," said Liberty.

"Don't think you're special just because this is your last year."

"Don't worry. You'll be there next year." Liberty left the room.

Today was the first day of school. It was also Liberty's senior year and Freedom's junior year. Junior year meant one thing. That senior year was close behind. Soon Liberty would be leaving for collage and Freedom would be moving into her final year of high school.

Although the thought excited her it also made her sad. It was going to be weird not seeing Liberty walking the halls of their high school. Next year she was going to have to navigate senior year without her best friend close by.

Even worse, Liberty probably wouldn't have time for her once she started college. Freedom was going to have to savor the remaining time they had.

She was going to have to think about what was going to happen next year, later. She had to pull herself from her thoughts and focus back on the light switch.

It moved without her touching it. She was sure of it. This was more exciting than junior year.

She loved all things supernatural. One of her favorite characters was Bonnie from *The Vampire Diaries.* She watched other things too but if it had anything to do with the supernatural you could almost bet that she's either seen or read it.

Freedom took a deep breath. Focusing on the light switch, she wanted to see if she could make it do what she wanted.

Turn off.

The switch obeyed and moved to the OFF position. She nearly jumped up and down from excitement, but remembered that she was not alone in the apartment. She didn't want to draw any attention to herself.

She reigned in her happiness and took a deep breath.

Turn on.

Again the switch obeyed and the light turned back on.

Isis stepped into the doorway.

"Don't even think about turning that light off," she said.

Freedom looked at her guiltily. Could Isis know what she was able to do?

"Stop trying to get back in the bed and get ready for school," said Isis.

"Liberty's in the bathroom," she said. Freedom hoped that her voice didn't betray guilt. She felt like she had just been caught with her hand in the cookie jar.

"Okay, so get your things ready so when she's done you can get right in," said Isis.

"Okay."

Isis didn't move from her spot in the doorway. Freedom put her hands up in surrender and walked over to the closet. She couldn't see Isis but she could feel her still watching, so she opened the door and took out her outfit for the day. It was a uniform. It was always a uniform. The same uniform Liberty will be wearing as well as everyone else at school.

One side of the closet held their uniforms while the other side held their regular clothes. Freedom took one of the uniforms out and laid it across the bed. Isis turned and left the room. While Liberty was in the shower, Freedom decided she would brush her teeth. Plus, she really had to use the bathroom.

She stepped into the bathroom and was engulfed in steam. Liberty liked her showers hot and there always seemed to be a lot of steam in the bathroom.

"Who's there?" Liberty called out.

"It's me. I have to use the bathroom," Freedom responded

"Kay. Just don't flush the toilet when you're done."

"I would be surprised if you could even tell the difference."

"Trust me. I can tell."

"Are you nervous or excited?" Freedom asked.

"About?" Liberty asked.

"The first day of school."

"I guess a little bit of both. Why?"

"I don't know. I was thinking about how you aren't going to be there next year."

Liberty didn't say anything for a minute. "You're going to be fine." Was all she said.

Freedom stepped over to the sink. She couldn't help but think about flushing the toilet. Unfortunately that was all it took. The toilet responded by flushing. Liberty screamed.

"Freedom!" She yelled.

"Oh God! I'm sorry."

The steam rose. Freedom felt like she was in a sauna. It didn't seem normal.

The steam started to dissipate.

"Are you okay?" Freedom asked.

"Yeah. Are you done? I'm gonna get out," Liberty said. She sounded calmer.

"I'm leaving."

Freedom stepped out of the bathroom to allow Liberty to get out of the shower.

Jonah stepped into the hall.

"Who's in there?" she asked, looking at the bathroom door.

"Liberty."

Jonah sighed and walked into the kitchen.

The bathroom door opened and Liberty emerged wrapped in a towel.

"Were you trying to give me third degree burns?"

"I said I was sorry. Besides the water couldn't have been that hot."

Liberty walked down the hall towards their room. Freedom didn't understand how the water could heat up like that. She didn't have time to think about it.

LIBERTY

—

60

September 5, 2014
6:40 AM

Liberty stood under the showerhead. Today was her first day of her final year of high school. She was looking forward to getting back to school and to the freedom that came with being a senior.

The door opened.

"Who's there?" Liberty called out.

"It's me. I have to use the bathroom," Freedom said.

"Kay. Just don't flush the toilet when you're done," Liberty said.

"I would be surprised if you could even tell the difference," Freedom said.

"Trust me, I can tell."

"Are you nervous or excited?" Freedom asked.

"About?" Liberty asked.

"The first day of school."

"I guess a little bit of both. Why?"

"I don't know. I was thinking about how you aren't going to be there next year."

Liberty understood what Freedom was feeling. They took different classes but she was always around whenever Freedom needed someone to talk to. That was going to change.

"You're going to be fine," Liberty finally said.

Liberty stepped under the water to rinse off and it scorched her skin. She let out a scream.

"Freedom!"

"Oh God! I'm so sorry," Freedom said.

She stepped back from the water. *Cool down.* The steam in the bathroom started to thin. She hesitantly placed her hand under the water. It's returned to the temperature that she preferred.

"Are you okay?" Freedom asked.

"Yeah. Are you done? I'm gonna get out."

"I'm leaving," Freedom said.

Liberty stepped back under the water and let it run over her body. She only remained in the shower for a few minutes before she wrapped a towel around her body and stepped out.

Liberty walked into the girl's bathroom. Senior year had given her a schedule that was full of freedom. She still had her mandatory classes but she had a lot more free time on her hands. Her fifth and sixth period were completely free and seventh was for lunch. She could pretty much do what she wanted as long as she stayed out of the halls.

Standing in front of one of the three sinks were two of her classmates, Cierra and Vanessa. They were taking pictures.

Senior year had just begun and already everyone was taking way more pictures than usual. She didn't want to stop because she really had to use the bathroom but they called her name.

"Liberty. Take a picture with me," Cierra said.

Reluctantly, she walked over and posed for pictures with both girls.

They took several pictures before Vanessa said, "We have to get back to class."

"Okay. I have this and next period free," Liberty said.

"Damn. Why didn't I get that schedule?" Cierra asked.

"You probably have to have grades like Liberty to get that schedule," Vanessa said.

"Well, damn," Cierra said.

The girls left the bathroom.

Liberty didn't consider herself to be super smart or anything. It was just important for her to get good grades. She felt the need to live up to the accomplishments of her sisters. Genesis had been studying pre-law before their lives had changed. Isis had stopped short of becoming a doctor and Jonah had started with sociology courses.

Things had changed for them ten years ago but it hadn't changed the fact that her sisters had been good enough to all get accepted into the college of their choice. She felt like she had to live up to that. So, she studied and worked hard.

Liberty stepped over to the sink after she walked out of the stall. As she reached for the handle, the water began to run in the sink. She quickly moved her hand back. She stared at the sink and the running water. *The sink must be broken.* She figured she would tell the office administrator on her way back to the library.

63

She stepped over to the other sink and reached for the handle. Just like with the first sink, the water turned on before she touched it. She moved to the last sink. As with the other two, the water turned on before she touched the handle.

She stepped back and stared at the three sinks. Behind her she heard the water in the toilets running. It sounded like someone had flushed all five but she was alone in the bathroom.

Liberty was trying not to panic but it was hard not to when things were suddenly turning on. *I wish all of this water would stop.* All at once, the water in the faucets stopped running and the toilets were silent.

She looked around the bathroom. She walked over to one of the sinks. She reached for the handle and the water started to flow from the faucet. She moved her hand away and it stopped. Realization hit her. *I'm doing this.* She was no longer freaking out.

Liberty stared at the faucet. "Turn … on," she said in an attempt to see if she could do it again. Nothing happened.

She sighed, *Now the water won't turn on.* Instantly the water started to flow. *Hmm.* When she had tried to get the water to turn on it didn't, but when she wasn't trying it did.

She turned the handle to the OFF position but the water continued to flow. The handle was already off and it wouldn't budge. She tried the other handle and it didn't work. She started to panic again.

She tried the handles again. It didn't work. "Stop!" she yelled. Nothing. *Why won't this water just stop?* The water immediately turned off.

Se heard the bell ring, signaling the end of fifth period. She took out her cellphone and sent a text. *Meet me n the girl's bathroom by the library. Now.*

Liberty didn't know what was going on but she needed to talk to her best friend right now.

Maybe she could try and convince her that she was not crazy.

She knew she wasn't crazy. She had watched all of the water turn on without any help from her.

There was just the fact that there was nobody there to witness it.

If she told anyone else they would think she was crazy. There was only one person she could tell.

Chapter 6: Freedom

Freedom stood outside of her fifth period class. Two of her best friends waited with her.

"I wish they had called school off today," Tanedra said. Tanedra was a mocha colored black girl. She recently cut off all of her hair and wore it in a short style similar to Fantasia from American Idol. "Who starts back to school on a Friday?"

"I almost didn't come today. My mom thought it was stupid," Hayden said. Hayden was a petite white girl with really long blond hair.

"That's because it is stupid," said Tanedra.

"Well at least your mom considered letting you stay home. My sister's would never let me miss school," Freedom said.

The bell sounded and she jumped. Her cell phone fell from her hands. *Please don't hit the floor.* The phone seemed to stop just inches before it crashed to the floor. Before anyone else could notice, she bent down and picked up the phone.

"Good reflexes," Hayden said.

"Yeah." Is all she could manage to say. They didn't seem to notice that the phone hovered above the floor.

———

TaQuanda Taylor
They entered the classroom as the bell finished sounding.

Freedom walked over to her desk and her seat pulled out before she touched it. She looked around to see if anyone was watching. No one seemed to be paying attention to her so she took a seat.

History had to be the most boring class that was ever created. At least it was in her opinion. She could care less about what happened hundreds of years ago.

The teacher, Mrs. Devine, passed out a sheet that listed everything they were going to need for class. Notebooks, binders, pens, pencils. It was pretty much the same list she'd gotten from all of her other classes.

She heard about Mrs. Devine from Liberty who had her class last year. She wasn't the type of teacher that would give them a break just because it was the first day of school. And it didn't matter that the first day of school landed on a Friday either.

Attendance had been taken. The supplies list had been passed out. Now, students were taking history books and passing them back so that everyone would have one.

Freedom looked down at her book once it was placed on her desk. *American History.* She groaned silently. She couldn't wait for the day when she no longer had to take this class or any that was even remotely similar.

"Do not open your books. These are yours for this year." Mrs. Devine said.

Freedom watched the teacher go to the front of each row and place a stake of papers on the first desk.

"Take one and pass it back." Mrs. Devine said.

Once the paper made it to her desk she looked down at it. *Dang it.* It's a test.

"You guys can go ahead and start the test. There is no pass or fail. I just want to know where you are."

Why do teachers always do this? Was it really important to quiz your students to find out what they already knew? Freedom didn't know much. She wondered what would happen if she failed the test. Mrs. Devine couldn't seriously start teaching her differently. That would totally single her out.

Because she didn't believe teachers could really do that, she believed these tests were pointless.

She reached into her purse and pulled out a pencil. Freedom wrote her name and the date at the top of the page and then put the pencil down.

She stared at the test. Everything looked like gibberish. It wasn't like she couldn't read. She could read just fine. It was because she never understood history, so nothing on the paper made sense to her.

Freedom sat back in her chair and stared at her pencil. She watched enough supernatural movies and TV shows and whenever a girl could do something with her mind she always spun a pencil on her desk.

She knew that she was not going to do well on the test. She contemplated not even taking it.

Freedom stared at her pencil. *Spin.* The pencil didn't move. *Spin.* It rocked slowly and then started to rotate on her desk. She put her finger over the pencil being sure not to touch it. She moved her finger in a circular motion. The pencil followed the direction of her finger and began to spin faster.

She didn't realize that Mrs. Devine had walked over to her, because she was so engrossed in what she was making the pencil do, until she spoke.

"Miss. Battle?" Mrs. Devine called her name.

Freedom jumped and slammed her hand on top of the pencil. She looked up and met her teacher's eyes.

"Yes?"

"Please do stop playing with your pencil and take your test. Remember you can't pass or fail it. I just want to know what you know." Mrs. Devine smiled kindly at her.

"Okay."

Mrs. Devine walked away and Freedom watched her go. She wondered if she had seen what she was doing.

She had been standing so close while Freedom was spinning the pencil, but she didn't say anything. All she had said was to stop playing with it. Maybe that was all it had looked like to her. Freedom looked around to see if anyone else had been watching her.

Everyone was looking down at their tests. No one seemed to have noticed.

Maybe they couldn't see what she could do. In the hall when she had stopped her phone from falling, all that her friends had noticed was that she had caught the phone. Now Mrs. Devine had been standing over her while she spun her pencil without touching it, but she didn't seem to see that last part. She just saw the pencil spinning. She probably thought her finger had been touching it the entire time.

Freedom picked up her pencil to take her test.

———

Mrs. Devine said it didn't matter whether she passed or failed so she just answered the questions about America's history as best as she could.

"Pencil's down and pass your test to the front," Mrs. Devine said.

She managed to answer all of the questions. Whether she answered them correctly would remain a mystery.

She handed the paper to the boy sitting in front of her, who in turn handed both to the person in front of him.

Mrs. Devine collected all of the tests and made it back to her desk.

"There will be no homework. You guys can enjoy your weekend," said Mrs. Devine.

That surprised her. She was sure they would have been assigned some reading from the thick hardcover book.

The bell began ringing signaling the end of fifth period. Her phone vibrated at that moment. She took the phone out before collecting her things and looked at the text message. It was from Liberty: *Meet me n the girl's bathroom by the library. Now.*

She collected her things and hurried out of the classroom.

"Hey where are you going? The cafeteria is this way." Tanedra pointed in the opposite direction from where she had been headed.

"I'm not going to lunch. I'm going to find Liberty." Liberty's message sounded urgent.

"Everything okay?" Hayden asked.

"Yeah. I'll see you guys seventh period" Freedom hurried away before they could ask her anything else. She had one thing on her mind. *Get to Liberty.*

Freedom walked into the bathroom and found Liberty standing in front of the window.

"What's up?" she asked, trying not to sound worried. Liberty was about her complexion, which was dark brown, but she somehow looked lighter right now. What could be bothering her?

Liberty didn't say anything. She just motioned for her to come here. She walked over to her and sat her things down on the floor.

"Is something wrong?" Freedom asked.

"Wait," said Liberty.

They both relaxed against the window. They stood in silence for a moment as girls entered and exited the bathroom.

"You have lunch this period right?" Liberty asked.

Freedom looked over at her. Liberty stared straight ahead.

"Yeah," she said. "Free period?"

"Yeah," Liberty answered. She was still facing forward.

The bell sounded, signaling the start of sixth period. The bathroom cleared out. Liberty finally turned to face Freedom.

"Okay, so I went to wash my hands and the water came on," said Liberty.

"Okay…" Freedom stared at her sister. She hoped that Liberty was feeling okay.

"I never touched the handle." Liberty said.

"Oh…" This entire time she had thought that she was alone in this whole supernatural-power-thing. It made more sense now if it was something that she shared with her sisters. "You mean like this."

Freedom thought it would be best to demonstrate. That way Liberty wouldn't think she was going crazy if she just blurted it out. Although, how could she think she was crazy when she just had her own supernatural experience. Freedom walked over to the closest of the three sinks in the bathroom and stood in front of it.

Freedom stared at the handle. *Turn.* Both handles on the sink slowly turn and the water turns on.

"I've been playing around with it today. I only wanted to turn the hot water on. I guess I haven't figured out-" Freedom stopped talking when she turned to look at Liberty.

Liberty was staring at the sink with her mouth open. Maybe Freedom had jumped the gun. Maybe Liberty couldn't do what she could and now she had just completely freaked her out.

Freedom looked from Liberty to the sink. Liberty had just seen what she could do unlike everybody else. Maybe that meant something.

Liberty walked over to the sink. Freedom stood quietly and watched as Liberty took in what had just happened. Freedom wasn't sure what she should say. She didn't know if she should try to explain what she had done. She didn't even know how to explain it.

"No," Liberty finally spoke. "Not like that." Liberty reached over and turned the handles to the OFF position, stopping the water. She looked over at Freedom.

Freedom held Liberty's gaze, even though she wanted to look away. "Um, so what were you talking about?" It was the only thing she could think to say.

"The handles didn't move," Liberty sounded calmer than Freedom thought she would have. "Not like they did just now."

"Show me again," said Liberty. Freedom didn't know what to do. Sure, Liberty sounded calm but she didn't look calm. "Free?" She shook herself back from her thoughts. "Show me again."

Freedom looked back at the sink. *Turn on.* Again both handles turn and the water begins flowing from the faucets. Once the water is on a thought crosses her mind.

"Did you wash your hands?" Freedom heard herself asking.

"Huh?" Liberty asked.

"Did you wash your hands?"

"No," answered Liberty. She walked over to the sink and thoroughly washed her hands. "I was going to but then all of the water in the bathroom started going crazy."

Freedom looked around the bathroom. "All of the water?" she asked.

"Yeah. The sinks and the toilets." Liberty dried her hands.

For some reason Freedom felt like she knew what happened, she just couldn't think of the name for it. She's read it in a book or seen it in a movie.

Freedom thought she knew exactly what Liberty could do.

Chapter 7: Liberty

Liberty was standing in front of the window when Freedom entered.

"What's up?" Freedom asked.

Liberty didn't say anything. She just motioned for Freedom to come over to her, which she did. Liberty didn't want to speak because what she had to say didn't need an audience and the bathroom was about to be flooded as girls made their way to their different classes.

"Is something wrong?" Freedom asked.

"Wait," Liberty said. She needed for them to be alone. She felt like if she started talking she might not be able to stop herself.

They relaxed at the same time. Having her sister near made her feel a little better. She felt Freedom's eyes on her but she didn't return her glance. Liberty just watched the girls flutter in and out of the bathroom.

They stood in silence for a moment as girls entered and exited the bathroom.

"You have lunch this period right?" Liberty asked.

"Yeah. Free period?" Freedom asked.

"Yeah." The bell sounded, signaling the start of sixth period.

The bathroom cleared out and Liberty turned to Freedom. "Okay, so I went to wash my hands and the water came on."

"Okay …" Freedom said. She was looking at Liberty like she was crazy. *Maybe I shouldn't have texted her.*

"I never touched the handle."

"Oh … You mean like this." Liberty watched as Freedom walked over to the sink that was closest to them.

Liberty was staring at Freedom trying to figure out what she was doing, that she almost missed actually seeing what she was doing. Liberty looked at the sink just in time to watch the handles turn and the water come on.

Liberty's mouth dropped open. She barely registered that Freedom was speaking. She was too busy staring in shock at the sink.

Liberty stepped over to the sink. She couldn't think straight. *What the heck just happened?* She saw it, but could she trust what she's seen?

"No. Not like that," she finally managed to get out. Liberty turned the handles, stopping the water and looked up at Freedom.

Freedom was making the face she had reserved for when she was caught doing something she was not supposed to be doing.

"Um, so what were you talking about?" she asked.

"The handles didn't move. Not like they did just now."

Liberty stared at her little sister and tried to make sense of what just happened.

"Show me again." Freedom didn't say anything. She just stared at Liberty. "Free," she tried using her sister's nickname to let her know everything was okay. "Show me again."

Freedom looked back at the sink and Liberty followed her gaze. She watched again as the handles turned and the water came on.

"Did you wash your hands?" Freedom asked out of nowhere.

"Huh?"

"Did you wash your hands?" Freedom asked again.

"No." Freedom looked down at the running water. Liberty knew what she was thinking. She took some soap and placed her hands under the water. It didn't turn off. She scrubbed her hands together under the water. "I was going to but then all of the water in the bathroom started going crazy." She was justifying, she knew.

Liberty looked up and saw that Freedom was looking around the bathroom.

"All of the water?"

Liberty wanted to know what Freedom was thinking.

"Yeah. The sinks and the toilets." Liberty grabbed some paper towels and dried her hands.

"Turn the water off." Freedom said. She sounded very calm. *I guess she would be calm considering what she can do.*

Liberty reached out for the handles.

"Not with your hands." Freedom stared at her.

"Then how am I supposed to turn it off?" Liberty knew the answer before the question left her mouth. Freedom answered anyway.

"The same way you got all of the water to come on."

Liberty knew she was going to say that. She looked at the water, at her sister and then back at the water. She took a couple of deep breaths trying to steady herself. She couldn't believe what she was about to try to do. Then again, if someone had told her what Freedom was able to do, she wouldn't have believed that either. She looked at the faucets and the handles trying to turn them off. Freedom walked over and stood next to her.

"You're trying to turn the handles aren't you?"

"Yeah."

"Stop."

"Then how am I supposed to turn off the water?" The water stopped.

They turn to look at each other. They turn back to the sink.

"Like that," Freedom said. She walked over to the sink and turned the handles to the OFF position. They move easily. "They were still on."

It took a minute but Liberty finally caught on. She watched the same movies and read the same books that Freedom had.

"So if I want the water on-" Liberty stopped mid sentence. The water came on. "And if I want it off ..." The water stopped.

They each had a spot in front of two of the three sinks. Neither of them had a class to be at. Freedom said she didn't mind missing lunch. Learning that they could do things with their minds had been the most exciting thing to happen to them in a long while. Now they both stood trying to practice their new … abilities.

Liberty was trying to command the water to turn on. The water turned on just as easily as it had when she hadn't been trying.

Freedom stood at the sink to her left. She was trying to get one handle to turn at a time. They both turned every time.

Freedom turned to look at her. "Guess I still need some practice."

"Try thinking about which handle you want to turn."

"I am," Freedom said. Liberty watched as she turned back to the sink.

Liberty could tell that Freedom was getting frustrated. Freedom lifted her hand and mimicked turning the handle.

The handle controlling the hot water on all three sinks turn. She turned to look at Liberty. "Close enough."

"Do you think it's weird that we're not freaked out about this?" Liberty asked. Liberty stopped the water in all three sinks.

"Nope. I think secretly every girl wishes she had a power. At least I've always wanted one. Now I have it."

The bell rang signaling the end of sixth period.

"Meet you out front after school," Liberty said.

"Yeah," Freedom responded. She collected her things.

TaQuanda Taylor

They exit the bathroom together. Liberty headed towards the library to get her things so she could get to lunch. She was starving and felt bad that Freedom had missed lunch.

A girl was in front of the water fountain. The water was pumping out very low. The girl looked like she was contemplating on whether or not she wanted to lean close for a drink.

Liberty thought about the water pressure increasing and like magic it did. The girl leaned in and drank from the fountain. Magic. That's exactly what it was. There was no other way to explain it. She didn't know why it was happening but she liked it.

Her phone buzzed and she took it out of her pocket. She looked down at the text message from Freedom: *Saw that.* ☺. Liberty smiled and looked over her shoulder. Freedom was standing outside of the bathroom smiling. She smiled back and stepped into the library. *This is going to be fun.*

Liberty went to collect her things and stopped.

She didn't know what was happening to her and Freedom. She was wondering if it was happening to the rest of them too. She didn't even know what to call it.

The idea that she was able to control water was thrilling. If anyone had ever said that they had never wanted to have power, they would probably be lying.

How many times did you have a conversation with someone and wish that you could read their mind to find out what they were really thinking? There were probably a number of things that people wished they could do that just didn't seem possible and she could do one of them.

The student in her had to know more.

This was technically a free period because it was just lunch. She had permission to leave school during lunch. This wasn't Sunnydale High, so she doubted she would find what she needed in this library.

Liberty figured that she would leave school and head to the Brooklyn library. Hopefully there she could find a book, any book that would help her understand more.

Liberty collected her things and left the school library.

Liberty caught the bus over to the library. It took some time to get there so she had to hurry if she was going to make it back to school for eighth period and her last class of the day. She had nothing to do for three periods but if she missed this one she would probably get into trouble. She didn't want to think about what Genesis would say if she did get into trouble.

Liberty looked through the computer catalog trying to find the right book. She didn't know what she was looking for so she tried a bunch of different keywords. She stopped looking when she came across a book about witches and powers. It was like a witch dictionary. Something was telling her that this was the book she needed.

She wrote down the book location and went to search for it.

With her new book in hand Liberty walked back through the doors of the school. She got back just in time. She could hear the bell signaling eighth period. She made her way to her last class of the day. English.

Liberty decided to sit in the back of the class. She figured it would be easier to not pay attention and thumb through her book if she was not up front and center as usual.

She took her seat as the bell let everyone know they should be in class.

TaQuanda Taylor

Ms. Hannigan passed out a sheet letting them know what books they would be reading that year. She then passed around journals that they were supposed to write in everyday.

The main assignment for the day was to write a journal entry. They were to talk about what they did over the summer and what they expected out of senior year.

Liberty opened her journal and wrote the date at the top of the page.

September 5th, 2014.

She was all ready to start her first entry.

This summer I

Her attention was pulled to the book she checked out of the library on witchcraft. She knew she needed to focus but she really wanted to read the book.

She pulled her attention from the book and started writing her entry. While she was writing she found herself opening the book. It couldn't hurt to peek at it.

Liberty decided that she would write a little and then flip through the book a little. She would try to make herself do both.

She put her best multitasking skills to use and wrote her entry while flipping through the witchcraft book. She was so wrapped in doing both tasks that she almost missed the bell signaling the end of the day.

Chapter 8: Liberty

Liberty entered the apartment with Freedom close behind. They found Genesis and Isis sitting in the living room. Freedom stepped into the bedroom they shared, which was right off of the living room.

"What are you two drinking?" Liberty asked.

They were both sitting on the couch holding a glass.

"Grown up juice," Isis said. Which meant they were drinking wine.

Freedom returned and she was book-bag-less.

"Aren't you supposed to be at work?" Freedom asked Isis.

"Came home sick," Isis said.

Liberty and Freedom looked at each other and then at Isis. Liberty contemplated how to ask them if they had a superpower.

"What's going on?" Isis asked.

"What do you mean?" Liberty asked.

"I tell you I came home sick and neither of you ask me if I'm okay, so what's going on?" Isis asked again.

"I'd like to know the answer to that too," Genesis said. She sat her glass on the coffee table.

"Are you okay?" Freedom asked.

"Too late. Spill it," Isis said. Just like Genesis, she put her glass on the table.

"Um. Well," Liberty said. She didn't know what to say. It was easier having this conversation with Freedom.

"I'll just show them," Freedom said.

Freedom walked over to the TV and stared at the remote that was sitting on top of it.

"Show us what?" Isis asked.

"Just watch," Freedom said.

They both stared at Freedom. Liberty watched the remote. She knew what Freedom was about to do. She was about to move the remote with her mind. It would make any questions she wanted to ask them easier after they saw what Freedom could do.

The remote didn't move. Liberty knew her sister well enough to know that Freedom was going to get frustrated.

As if on clue, Freedom threw her arm out in aggravation that the remote did not moved.

The act of flinging her arm out sent the remote flying from the TV. It headed straight for Isis.

Isis screamed and threw her hands up to block her face. Then they were staring at an empty spot on the couch. Isis had disappeared.

Genesis jumped up from the couch. "Isis?!"

"In the kitchen!" Isis called out.

They ran from the living room.

When they stepped into the kitchen, Isis was standing in front of the refrigerator. Her hands were still up protecting her face.

"Whoa. You just teleported," Liberty said.

Isis lowered her hands a little. "What?"

"What exactly happened at work today?" Genesis asked.

"I was on the stairs and then I was in the locker room. I didn't know how I got there so I thought I blacked out or something," Isis answered.

"I'm guessing you did this little-trick today," Genesis said.

"Am I the only one who thinks this is cool?" Freedom asked.

"No. I'm right there with you sis," Liberty said.

"Well am I the only one who is freaked out?" Isis asked.

"Nope," Genesis responded.

"Really? You don't think this is cool?" Liberty turned to the sink. *Water turn on.*

The water obeyed her command and turned on. She looked over to see Isis gawking at the sink. Genesis had the same expression plastered on her face.

TaQuanda Taylor

Liberty didn't get it. Of course she had been freaked in the beginning but that hadn't lasted very long. She loved this new power. Her big sisters, however, did not look like they were enjoying it. In fact, they both looked like they could pass out at any moment.

She pulled out a chair and sat down. She took the book out of her bag.

"I got this book today and I've been going through it," Liberty said. She remembered that she had left the water on. Without turning back to the sink she said, "Stop water." The water obeyed.

Genesis dropped down in one of the other chairs.

"I didn't really know what I was looking for. I only had what Freedom and I could do to go off of."

Liberty opened the book and stopped at one of the pages she bookmarked.

"Freedom's power is called Telekinesis. Basically it means that she can control objects with her mind," Liberty said.

She didn't wait for anyone to say anything. Since she was already in the T's she flipped to TELEPORTATION.

"Isis your power is called Teleportation. It means you can move from one place to another without occupying any space in between."

"Which basically means that I'm not walking anywhere," Isis said.

"Basically." She didn't flip to hers because she's memorized it. "I'm called an Elemental. It was the only thing in here that could explain what I could do. What about you?" She asked Genesis.

"Huh?" Genesis asked.

"What can you do?"

"What's an Elemental?" Genesis asked.

Liberty knew that she was trying to change the subject and she let her.

"Basically It means I can control all of the elements. Water. Fire. Air. Earth and Spirit. I've only been able to control water so far."

"I need a glass of water," Isis said.

"Oh, okay. Water turn on."

Just like all of the other times the water listened and flowed from the faucet. Isis started to move to the sink.

"I got it," Freedom said, stopping her.

Freedom removed a glass from the dish rack and held it under the water. She remained in the doorway so she was manipulating the glass with her mind. Once the glass was full it floated over to be eye level with Isis.

Isis stared at the glass.

"It's okay. Take the glass," Liberty said.

Isis reached out and wrapped her hands around the glass. She moved her hand around the glass as if she were looking for strings. Liberty laughed.

Isis put the glass to her lips and greedily drank all of the water. She moved towards the sink.

"Want me to-" Freedom started.

"No I got it," Isis said. She put the glass in the sink.

TaQuanda Taylor

The water was still running and she tried to turn it off. It continued to run.

"Oh sorry. I keep forgetting that. You can stop now," Liberty said. The water stopped.

"I'll admit. That was kind of cool," Isis said.

"Told you," Freedom said.

"And still a little freaky," Isis countered.

"And to think that you backed away from me earlier," Genesis said to Isis.

"I've already apologized for that. It was reflex. I didn't mean to," Isis said.

"What's going on?" Liberty asked them.

"Nothing." They said in unison.

"Where did you get this book from?" Genesis asked.

"Brooklyn public library."

"When did you have time to go to the library? Weren't you supposed to be in school today?"

"I was in school but I had some free periods."

"I want to take a look at your class schedule again," Genesis said.

"Why are we even talking about this? We have supernatural powers."

Liberty didn't understand how Genesis could find now to try and reprimand her for skipping out on school. More important things were happening at the moment.

Liberty liked the fact that they were not freaking out but at the moment they were not really expressing any emotion.

This was a big deal and she wanted to deal with it now, not her class schedule. Not only did they have to figure out what everyone could do but the next step was to figure out why they could do it.

Chapter 9: Jonah

Jonah walked into the apartment. She instinctively turned into the living room. That was where she had expected to find her sisters, seated around the TV. When she stepped in she noticed it was uncharacteristically empty.

"Where is everybody?" she called out.

"In the kitchen!" Genesis said.

Jonah turned out of the living room and made the small trip to the kitchen.

She found all of her sisters there, including Isis who should have been at work.

"Why are you all squeezed in here?" she asked. The kitchen was small which was normal for a Brooklyn apartment. "And what are you doing home?" she asked Isis.

"I thought I was having blackouts," Isis said. Her always light complexion looked pale.

"You 'thought' you were having blackouts?" Jonah tried, unsuccessfully, to keep the worry out of her voice.

"Yeah. But don't worry, I was just teleporting," Isis said sarcastically.

Jonah's worries dissolved into confusion. She stared at her older sister by two years, trying to figure out if she was trying to pull a prank on her. Before she could speak, Liberty did.

"Did anything … weird happen to you today?"

"Besides this conversation? No." Jonah answered.

Jonah remembered her earlier concerns.

"Why were you in the hospital today and why didn't you answer my calls?"

"You were in the hospital?" Liberty and Freedom asked in unison.

"You called her?" Genesis turned to Isis.

"Of course. I wasn't going to worry alone," Isis answered.

"Well?" Jonah pried.

"I had to get checked out after I fell over a banister." Genesis said nonchalantly.

Her careless tone wasn't enough to stop the three of them from freaking out.

"Okay. Okay. Calm down. I didn't get hurt," Genesis said.

"What do you mean you didn't get hurt?" Jonah asked.

"She magically healed herself," Isis said. Genesis turned to look at her. "If I'm going to freak out about having a supernatural power, so are you." Isis turned to look at Jonah. "Jo, we were talking about all of the weird things that happened to us today."

"Weirder than this moment right now?" Jonah asked.

"Well ... yeah," Isis said.

"Blackouts and super healing? This is what you all were talking about?" Jonah asked.

"Not a blackout. She was teleporting," Liberty said. She turned to look at Genesis. "You healed yourself?"

"That's what she did," Isis said. "She had bruises on her neck cause the guy she arrested choked her. She had a cut on the back of her neck from the fall. She doesn't have any broken bones and she was shot. Four times."

Freedom moved to Genesis and looked at her neck. "I don't see anything."

"That's cause they disappeared when we were in the living room," said Isis.

"Wow. You really healed yourself?" Freedom asked. She sounded amazed.

"Apparently," Genesis said.

Jonah stood in the doorway of the kitchen staring at her sisters. Maybe they all had the same illness that made them imagine things. What they were talking about didn't make sense. More importantly it was impossible.

"Are you guys okay?"

"Nothing happened to you today?" Genesis asked.

"No. I didn't 'teleport' or 'heal myself' or anything." Jonah answered using air quotes to show how ridiculous they sounded.

"Well it wouldn't be the same thing that we can do. We all can do different things so you would have a different power," Freedom said.

Jonah looked around the kitchen. "I get it now."

"Get what?" Liberty asked.

"I get what's going on?"

"Really?" Liberty asked.

"Yeah. It's the ten-year anniversary of the day mom left."

She didn't exactly leave. She had no choice.

Jonah turned her attention to Freedom. "It's not important how she left, it's the fact that she's gone. It's an important part of our lives. Your mind's must have somehow created this delusion that you all have inhuman abilities as a way to deal with today."

Freedom's face scrunched up like she was trying to figure something out.

"But you're immune to it?" Liberty asked.

"Well yeah. I don't feel the same way you guys do about her leaving."

Great she's trying to shrink us. Hello you didn't even finish school. You have no idea what you're talking about.

"No, I didn't finish school but I'm also not the one standing here pretending I have 'powers'," Jonah said. She looked at Isis. "I can't even believe you would throw that in my face."

Isis' mouth dropped open. "S-sorry," she stammered.

Genesis stood. "No one is saying anything about you not finishing school."

"Yes she did. She just said it," Jonah pointed to Isis.

They look from Jonah to Isis. She didn't know why they looked so confused.

"I didn't say it," Isis said.

"Yes you did. I heard you. You said I didn't know what I was talking about because I didn't finish school," Jonah said. She hoped that her voice didn't betray the fact that her feelings had been hurt.

"Jo, I didn't say it. I thought it," Isis said.

They all turned to look at Jonah.

"What?" Jonah asked.

"Everything that you heard never left my mouth. It wasn't meant for you to hear," Isis said. She looked really sad. "I'm sorry but it's what I was thinking."

Jonah stared at Isis but everyone was staring at Jonah.

"You heard me think about mom not leaving us didn't you? That's why you looked at me," Freedom said.

Jonah turned to look at her.

"Guess that something 'weird' is happening to you," Freedom said.

Jonah walked into the living room with her sisters close on her tail.

"Jo you can read minds. Again sorry. I'm really sorry about that. I seem to be offending sisters left and right today." Isis said.

TaQuanda Taylor
This is so cool. Freedom.

Why didn't I get mind reading? I could've really used that today.
Genesis.

This is unbelievable. I wonder if she's reading my mind right now.
Hi Jo. Liberty.

I really didn't mean it the way it sounded. I promise. Isis

Jonah threw her hands over her ears and whirled around. "Would
you all just shut up?" She screamed.

"We didn't say-" Genesis started and then stopped. *You're reading*
our minds, aren't you?

Jonah glared at her. Genesis mouthed 'I'm sorry'. Jonah dropped
down on the couch.

"Why is this happening?" She said. She wanted to cry. Her sister's
thoughts were starting to give her a headache.

"Do you still think our minds is playing tricks on us because we're
sad about mom?" Liberty asked. She sat down beside her. *Sad isn't*
exactly what I would call how you feel about mom.

Jonah turned to look at her. "Can you please not think?"

"Sorry. It's hard not to. Especially because I know that I never have
to open my mouth around you ever again," Liberty said.

"All of your thoughts are giving me a headache," Jonah said.

"Okay, we'll try not to... think," Isis said. She made a face as if she
was trying to figure out if what she had just said made any sense.

———

"Not really," Jonah replied, looking at her.. "But when you are dealing with someone who can hear your thoughts it makes perfect sense."

"So you heard that?" Isis asked.

"Yup," Jonah said. "I don't want this. I mean maybe if I was still in the ninth grade and I was trying to figure out if Anthony Daniels liked me, but not now."

She put her head in her hands. She felt like her head was going to explode.

"Are you okay?" Genesis asked.

"Did you say that or think it? I can't tell the difference." Jonah said, head still down.

"I said it," Genesis said.

Liberty was sitting on her right so Genesis sat down on her left. She began rubbing a small circular pattern on her back. Jonah looked up.

"I'm confused," Jonah finally admitted. Being able to read her sister's minds had her freaked out for a second. Now that second had come and gone and all she was left with was confusion.

Jonah rolled her eyes. "You would think that wouldn't you?"

"Well you were the one who brought it up and it makes sense," Genesis said.

"Hey for the ladies who can't read minds can you tell us what you're talking about?" Isis asked.

"She thinks we should go talk to mom," Jonah said.

Jonah looked at her sisters as they all silently agreed.

———

"I thought you were going to try not to think?" Jonah said and sat back.

"But you honestly can't expect us to stop all of our thoughts?" Freedom asked.

"You know what? You're absolutely right. There's no way I can stop you from thinking."

So what does it feel like? Freedom.

"I can't stop you from thinking but I can get away from it." Jonah stood and headed towards the door.

"Where are you going?" Genesis asked.

"I need some air. I can't deal with all of this right now." Jonah left the apartment.

They may all be cool with this but Jonah just couldn't take it. It's all too weird. Hearing people's thoughts. Sure it sounded cool in a snooper kind of way but on a normal level it was just weird.

Plus she was still a little hurt from Isis' comment or thought. Whatever. She just needed to walk it off.

Jonah didn't have any specific location in mind. She just needed to walk. She needed some time to clear her head and get away from her sisters thoughts.

This 'power' or whatever it was made her feel like she was intruding on their private thoughts. Granted so far they've only been thinking about these new events.

But what happened when the excitement faded and they were thinking about something they wanted to keep private? She was going to feel like she was invading their privacy.

Nobody should be able to just pry on people whenever they want to.

Why should she be able to?

A man walked in her direction. She wanted to turn and walk in the opposite direction.

If she was going to be able to do this she might as well get used to it.

Jonah braced herself as they passed each other.

Nothing. She didn't get so much as a blip.

How is that possible? Maybe she couldn't really read minds. Maybe she was imagining the whole thing.

Jonah pinched herself to make sure she was awake. *Ouch.* Didn't dream it. Plus, she still had the headache from when her sister's thoughts had invaded her head.

Chapter 10: Eve

September 6, 2014

Eve opened her eyes and stared up into darkness. She lightly pressed her fingers to her lips, remembering a kiss that still lingered. The small slot in her door opened.

"Battle, you have a visit." The voice came from the other side of the door.

She got up from the cot and walked over to the door. Eve placed both of her hands through the slot. Metal was secured around her wrists. She pulled her hands back and she was wearing a pair of handcuffs.

The door opened and a female corrections officer was waiting on the opposite side. Eve stepped out of the room and the door slammed shut behind her.

She was led down a long corridor. This was a walk that she had done many times over the last ten years. Many times it was because she was getting the chance to see her daughters. Other times it was because her lawyer had news for her. She wondered which it was today.

Eve stepped up to a large white door. The CO unlocked the door and opened it. She stepped through the door. She was in a large plastic box. Sitting on the other side of the barrier were her daughters. She counted five faces. She couldn't help but smile. Jonah had finally come for a visit. Today was going to be a good day.

TaQuanda Taylor

It had been a long time since she had seen all five of her girls.

The door closed and she heard the lock click. Eve turned to the door and slide her hands through the opening. The handcuffs were removed. She turned back to her girls and her smile faltered. *No. It can't be.* Jonah didn't come visit her because she missed her. She had to come. They all did.

Eve recovered herself and sat down on the waiting stool.

"Hi girls." She didn't know if she should bring up the elephant in the room or let them do it. She hadn't been expecting this. Eve spent her entire life hoping that this would never happened.

"Hi mom." They each said. Except for Jonah. Jonah had been watching Eve intently since she stepped into the plastic box.

"Jonah." Eve spoke solely to her. Still nothing.

It was not like she expected her to be all warm and fuzzy. There was a lot of unfinished business between the two of them.

They watched each other for a while. If she didn't say anything they would be sitting here like this for the whole visit.

"You're not going to be able to read my mind." Eve said to Jonah.

Jonah's mouth dropped open in shock.

"Mom?" Genesis grabbed her attention. "You want to tell us what's going on?"

Eve was not ready for this. She turned her attention back to Jonah.

"It's been a long time."

"Ten years," Jonah said.

"Mom?" Genesis called to Eve.

Eve turned her attention back to her eldest. Genesis was the strong one. The leader. The protector. Her child blessed with the power to stop harm inflicted on herself and those around her.

"One word. Witch." Eve didn't want to have this conversation. Why didn't she pick up on the signals before? Maybe she could have prepared herself for this visit. Right now, she didn't want to speak about it.

"What?" Genesis.

"Witch?" Isis.

"This is for real?" Liberty.

"Cool." Freedom.

Going down the line she answered all of their questions. Including Jonah's unspoken one.

"You're witches. Yes. Yes. It can be cool. All of your lives."

"So you can-?" Jonah stopped herself. She couldn't voice it out loud.

"You can't read mine but I can read yours."

"What's going on?" Genesis asked.

"We're just talking that's all," Eve answered.

"I think it's time to start freaking out," Genesis said.

"Right there with you sis," Isis said.

"What do you girls feel? Right here, with me?" Eve asked them all.

"Freaked," Genesis said.

"With you again," Isis added.

"Normal," Liberty said.

"Power," Jonah said.

Eve looked at Jonah.

"What are you talking about?" Genesis asked.

"I feel power. Like, a lot of power. It's coming from you isn't it?" Jonah asked.

"Yes it is," Eve answered.

"What is she-" Genesis is cut off.

"Whoa," Freedom said. "That's coming from you? Man, if you weren't my mother and I wasn't sitting beside my big sister's I would have a few expletive words to say."

"You did say it." Jonah said to Freedom.

"Oh, yeah. Sorry about that," Freedom said. "But I didn't know what that feeling was earlier. It feels good, really good. It also feels comforting."

"That's what that is?" Genesis asked.

"Yes. You can feel my power. How does that make you feel?" Eve asked.

"Like I don't want to freak out," Genesis replied.

"It feels right. Like this is how it's supposed to be," Liberty said.

Eve looked down at her hands. *Deep breath.* She looked back up. "That's because this is how it's supposed to be," Eve said.

"You're not really telling us anything," Jonah said.

Eve turned to look at Jonah. She was glad that Jonah couldn't read her mind.

"Jo, she just told us we're witches," Isis whispered.

"There's more, I feel it," Jonah said.

"You're right. I am keeping something from you." Eve was not interested in having this conversation. She gave Jonah information but it was not what she was keeping secret. "You haven't received your power."

"But she can read minds," Isis said.

"Yes, she can read your minds, but that isn't her gift. That's just a part of it," Eve said.

"What is it?" Genesis asked.

"She'll get it. In due time, " Eve said.

"This is so unbelievable," Liberty said.

"And yet very believable," Isis said.

"Okay, let's talk about something else," Eve said.

"I think we should talk about this," Genesis said.

"No, we shouldn't. There are microphones here and I've already said too much."

TaQuanda Taylor

"Oh. Okay. Yeah. We'll talk about something else," Genesis said.

"So, Liberty, How is senior year going?" Eve asked.

"We'll we've only been back to school one day so not much happened," Liberty answered.

Eve turned to Jonah. Right now Eve wished Jonah could read her mind. If Jonah weren't so closed off to Eve she would hear Eve asking her to drop it.

"Oh. Okay. Have you thought about college?"

"Yeah. I think I want to go to NYU but Genesis wants me to go out of state."

"Everybody should get the change to go away for college. I tried to get Isis and Jonah to go away too," Genesis said.

"I feel like you're always trying to get rid off us," Isis said.

"That's because I am," Genesis laughed.

They sat and talked for hours about what's been going on with them since their last visit. Jonah didn't join in the conversation but that didn't mean she hadn't talked. She spent the entire visit talking to Eve through her thoughts. Eve glanced at her repeatedly trying to let her know that she was not saying anything further.

The visit ended far too quickly. They say goodbye and the girls get up to leave.

"I'll see you again soon, Jonah," Eve said.

She turned to look at Eve. Her face was one giant question mark.

Yes, I will see you again soon. Real soon.

The door opened behind Eve. "Your lawyer is on his way in." The female CO said before slamming the door shut.

Eve expected this visit. She only wished it had come before her girls. She would have been better prepared for their visit.

Chapter 11: Eve

Ten Years Ago

Eve walked into the courtroom dressed sharply in a pants suit. Her wrists were handcuffed in front of her. Two officers, one in front and one in back, escorted her in. She's escorted over to the table known as the *Defendants Table.*

Sitting in the row behind the small barrier were her daughters, Genesis, 19, Isis, 17, Jonah, 15, Liberty, 7 and 6 year old Freedom.

Eve looked down into their confused faces. She pulled her attention away and turned to the officers. Her handcuffs were removed and she sat in the seat beside her attorney. Her attorney leaned over to discuss what will occur during their time in the courtroom.

Today the verdict will be read. It's taken the jury two days to come to a decision. Eve's informed that this is a good sign and that the verdict should go their way because it's taken them so long.

Eve sat up straight and looked around the courtroom. The D.A. filed in and took her place behind the desk opposite the one Eve occupied.

She turned around to face her girls. Eve plastered a smile on her face so that they wouldn't worry.

"Hey, why do you all look so sad?"

"I want you to come home," whined Freedom. She started to cry.

"I know baby. I want to come home too. Genesis why don't you take your sisters outside," Eve said.

"I'm staying," said Genesis. She looked worried.

"Isis?"

"I got it. Come on." Isis stood and waited for Liberty and Freedom to stand.

"Give me a hug."

Eve hugged the three off them before they vacated the row and left the courtroom. She turned her attention to Jonah who remained seated.

"Jo-"

Jonah stood without saying a word and left the courtroom. A part of Eve broke inside. She's never felt that amount of anger from Jonah before. She's not sure she will ever win her trust back.

"All rise for the Honorable Judge Wendy Jacobs," announced the bailiff.

Everyone in the courtroom rose to their feet. Judge Jacobs entered from her chambers and took her place at the bench. Once she was seated everyone followed suit and took theirs seats.

"Is the jury ready?" Judge Jacobs asked. The bailiff responded in the affirmative. "Bring them in."

The bailiff walked over to a door and opened it. Twelve men and women filed in and took their place in the jury box. Once they were all seated the Judge spoke again.

"Juror One, have you reached a verdict?"

A woman sitting in the first seat stood. She had curly blond hair and appeared to be in her early forties.

"We have Your Honor," she said. She never takes her eyes off of the judge.

The woman handed a folded piece of paper to the bailiff. Without opening the paper he handed it to the judge.

Judge Jacobs opened the paper and read the contents silently. She looked up at Eve and then down at the paper.

"Was this verdict unanimous?"

"Yes, Your Honor," said Juror One.

Judge Jacobs folded the piece of paper and handed it back to the bailiff, who in turn handed the paper to Juror One.

"Will the defendant please rise," said the bailiff.

Eve stood along with her attorney. She turned to look at Genesis. Genesis forced a smile. Eve turned her attention back to the jury. She knew the verdict before it was read. One of her many powers was the ability to read minds. She was more worried about what this would do to her family.

"Juror One will you please read the verdict," said Judge Jacobs.

Juror One opened the paper and read aloud. "In the case of the city of Philadelphia versus Eve Battle, the charge of Murder in the First Degree, we the jury find the defendant guilty."

Eve bowed her head. Knowing the verdict a head of time did not lesson the blow of hearing it read aloud. Her attorney placed his hand on her arm as a way to comfort her, but he couldn't comfort her. She didn't want her family ripped apart. She turned to look at Genesis and read the shock on her face.

Genesis sat with her mouth open. Neither of them said anything.

Eve was found guilty. She would be spending the rest of her life away from her daughters. They would probably be separated and put into foster homes.

It had been self-defense but she hadn't been able to prove it. Proving it would have ousted her as a witch. That was something she couldn't afford to do. It was a secret that she would have to take to her grave, just like those before her.

So, instead she told her lawyer what she could without giving away too much and prayed for the best. Unfortunately, her prayers had not been answered.

Eve turned back around when she noticed the officer in front of her.

"What's going on?" she asked.

She was so engrossed in her thoughts that she hadn't heard anything that was said.

"They're going to schedule your sentencing. Don't worry, we'll appeal it."

She was handcuffed and escorted out of the courtroom. She couldn't will herself to look back at her daughter.

Chapter 12: Jonah

Jonah exited through the prison door, her sisters followed behind. She couldn't believe that she had been talked into coming to this visit. The only thing she had learned was that her mom was still very much a liar.

Eve's leaving had always left her shaken up. She'd sworn ten years ago that she wouldn't get hurt like that again. Yet, she found herself sitting across from her mother listening to her lie. No good would ever come from trusting her.

Although Eve didn't give them much information, she knew that there was something else there. Just like she could feel her power she could feel that she was keeping something from them. *I'll see you again soon. Jonah.* Her words echoed in Jonah's head. What could she have been talking about? Eve could read Jonah's mind so she had to know that Jonah didn't want to come back.

"Jo, will you slow down?" Liberty asked.

Jonah didn't realize that she was walking fast. She stopped in the parking lot and turned to face her sisters who were a few feet behind her. She looked behind them at the prison and suddenly speeding away felt like the only thing she could do. She's never been here and she didn't want to come back.

"Are you okay?" Genesis asked.

"I'm fine," Jonah responded.

"You don't look fine," said Freedom.

Jonah stood in place staring at her sisters. They knew how much their mom's leaving had affected her. If she was being honest with herself, she always felt like Eve had abandoned them. She's never spoken the words out loud but she knew that her sisters could feel it.

"No, I'm not fine. I'm pissed," Jonah admitted.

"About what?" Isis asked.

Jonah walked over to her sisters so that she couldn't be overheard, even though they were the only ones in the parking lot. "She tells us we're witches, but that's it. She doesn't explain anything and to top it off she's hiding something."

She hated to admit it but she had thought that coming here would be a good idea. Maybe they would get some answers. All she felt though was the way she had felt ten years ago.

"She told us why we couldn't talk about it," Liberty said.

"That's B.S." Jonah said.

"No, it's not. They do record the visits. She can't say anything she can't explain later," Genesis said.

"What are you talking about? She had no problem blurting out that we're witches and asking us if we could feel her power. She only brought up that microphone thing when I questioned her." Jonah felt herself getting angry.

"No. When you questioned her she answered you. She said you didn't get your power," Liberty said.

Jonah wondered how it could be that she was the only one who could tell that Eve wasn't telling them everything.

"You guys seriously didn't feel it?" Jonah asked.

"Feel what? Her power? We all felt that," Isis said.

"No, you didn't feel like she was lying to us?" Jonah asked.

"What are you talking about?" Genesis asked.

"She was lying to us."

"Look, I don't think it's fair to accuse her of something when she can't defend herself," Freedom said.

"I'm not accusing her of anything," Jonah said.

"But you are." Freedom looked like she was trying to stop herself from getting upset. "You've hated her for ten years-"

"I don't hate her-"

"Yes you do," said Liberty. "She has been in here by herself for ten years. The only thing that probably keeps her from going crazy it that she can see her daughters and you've never even attempted to come here and see her."

"The one time you do visit, you accuse her of lying to us. It's like you think she's a monster or something." Freedom added.

"Look let's just all calm down," said Genesis.

"God! It's not that I'm accusing her of anything, it's that I'm the only one who can see her clearly."

"How do you know that's true?"

TaQuanda Taylor

Jonah looked at Isis. "What?"

"How do you know that you're the only one who can see her clearly? I mean you can't even read her mind." Isis said.

"Are you kidding me?" Jonah couldn't believe that her sisters were ganging up on her.

"I'm not trying to hurt your feelings. I just want to know if you think you can trust your own feelings. Maybe the years of feeling hurt and abandoned have clouded your judgment." Isis said.

Jonah didn't know what to say. True she's always felt abandoned and really hurt but her judgment wasn't clouded. Her sisters would never understand and now that she was the only one who could tell that everything had not been right about that visit, they won't understand.

"I don't know how to get you guys to understand. So, I'm not going to keep trying." Jonah turned and walked away.

Jonah wasn't paying attention to what was going on in front of her, so she didn't have time to move before she bumped into the stout man rushing towards the prison.

She was nearly knocked down from the impact of running into the man. She could faintly hear him utter 'sorry' before everything changed inside of her.

Jonah's chest started constricting. She felt like all of the air was slowly seeping from her lunges. She didn't have asthma but she suddenly felt like she was having an asthma attack. She was gasping for air when images began flashing through her mind.

She bent at the waist and put her hands on her knees. She tried taking small breaths. Her sisters were at her side. They sounded scared but she couldn't make out what they were saying. She knew that they were there but they felt like they were far away.

Just as quickly as the attack started, it ended. Her breathing returned to normal. Jonah straightened and turned to face the prison. The man had already disappeared inside, but she didn't really need to find him. She had a pretty good idea of who he was. She knew why he was there. And she knew without a shadow of a doubt that the power her mom said hadn't manifested had done just that.

"Jonah, are you okay?" She heard Genesis ask. Her voice sounded full of fear.

Jonah turned to face her sisters.

"I'm fine," Jonah said.

"What the hell happened?" Isis asked.

"I had an asthma attach," Jonah lied. She couldn't bring herself to tell them the truth.

"But you don't have asthma," Isis said.

"Asthma can always show up later in life though. Right?" Liberty asked.

"Yeah it can, but—that was bad Jo. I thought you were going to stop breathing." Isis said.

"I'm fine. Really. See, I'm breathing normal," Jonah said.

"Okay, but I would feel better if we could get to the hospital and maybe get you an inhaler. In case this happens again." Isis talked with ease, but she still looked shaken up.

"Yeah we can do that. Besides I have a feeling that will not be the last time." Jonah turned back to the prison in the direction the man went. *No, this is not the last time.*

TaQuanda Taylor

"Let's get back to New York and get you to the hospital." Genesis' voice broke through her thoughts.

"Yeah, we should go," Jonah turned back to her sisters. They were all staring at her.

They were all so scared and worried. They're thinking the same thing. They're thinking that Jonah had almost died. She wished she could prove to them that she was okay, but now wasn't the right time for that.

Chapter 13: Eve

Eve's visit with her lawyer was uneventful. What he told her, she already knew. Seeing her girls had told her everything she needed to know. Now she just needed to process it all.

She walked back towards her cell. The thought of sitting in that dark space suddenly depressed her. She needed air and some sunlight.

"Can I go outside?"

"You're not scheduled for yard time." The CO said.

Eve turned slowly to face the corrections officer. She made sure not to make a sudden move that would alarm the guard. Eve needed to make eye contact with her. She had many powers. She couldn't control minds but she could control moods. If done right it could be used as a mind control.

"I really don't want to go back to my cell." Eve's eyes locked onto the guards. She could feel her resolve loosening.

"I don't see what's wrong with you getting outside for a bit." The guard replied.

Eve stepped into the small square outdoor area she was allowed to visit one hour a week. There were four walls surrounding her but no roof.

TaQuanda Taylor

She looked up to the sky and closed her eyes. A single tear escaped and rolled down her cheek.

Eve walked quickly down a dark alley. It was raining softly.

"You can't run from me, Eve!"

She whirled around and stared at the man behind her. He was aiming a gun at her. She looked up at the sky. The clouds opened up and the rain fell harder. Eve looked back at the man. His vision was now impaired as he squinted against the rain.

"You know what will happen if you kill me."

"It's a price I'm willing to pay."

Eve watched as he pulled the trigger. She teleported and was standing behind him. He turned to try to shoot again. She flicked her wrist and he went flying across the alley and crashed on top of a large blue garbage can.

"You're not scheduled to be out here."

Eve opened her eyes and whirled around. A male corrections officer was standing in the doorway.

"Let's go. You're going back," he said.

JONAH

Jonah sat on the waiting exam table, while her sisters sat quietly around her. Well, they thought that they were being quiet.

"If you guys aren't going to say anything can you at least stop thinking it?" She asked. She knew they were scared but their thoughts were screaming at her.

"Sorry," they all murmured.

"You guys, I'm fine. It was just an asthma attack."

"Asthma attacks kill too, you know," said Isis.

"I know, but I'm fine. Trust me."

"I'll feel better after a doctor sees you," said Isis. Just then the door opened and the most gorgeous man Jonah thought she'd ever seen entered.

"Hi, I'm Dr. Taylor," he said. He looked down at the chart and then looked up. "Battle?" As if just realizing whose room he entered, "Isis, more family." His eyes lit up as they found Isis.

"Yeah, this is my little sister Jonah. Along with Liberty and Freedom and my older sister Genesis." She introduced them.

Jonah's head popped around and she gawked at Isis. Did she realize what she's thinking right now? Jonah looked over at Genesis. Apparently she was not the only one who thought Dr. Taylor was one good-looking man. Even Liberty and Freedom were thinking it, but Isis' thoughts were different.

"So Jonah, what seems to be the problem?" he asked.

"She had an asthma attack," Isis answered for her.

"How long have you had asthma?" he asked.

"Apparently since today," Jonah said.

"Have you ever been tested for it before?" he asked as he moved over to the cabinet behind her.

"No and I've never had an attack before."

Dr. Taylor returned with a small contraption. It had a tube with a ball at the bottom and attached to the top was a mouthpiece. He handed the device to Jonah.

"I want you to breath into this. Try to get the ball to the top. Big puffs," he said and stepped back.

Jonah placed the mouthpiece between her lips and breathed. The ball bounced to the surface. He didn't tell her to stop so she kept breathing. Isis walked over to stand by Dr. Taylor. They whispered among themselves.

"It doesn't appear that there is anything wrong with her breathing," he said.

Jonah watched Isis turn her attention back to her. Dr. Taylor took his stethoscope and placed it in his ears. He walked over to Jonah and placed the other part in the center of her back.

"Keep trying to get the ball to the top," he said.

She continued breathing into the device. While her sisters watched and Dr. Taylor listened to her breathing. He moved away from her and placed the stethoscope around his neck.

"I don't think you have asthma. The attack you had could have just been brought on by stress."

"Alex," Isis said but then corrected herself. "Dr. Taylor. Could you give her a prescription for an inhaler?"

"Isis, I don't believe there is any cause for that," he said.

"I know, but you didn't see this attack. If it happens again, I want her to be prepared" Isis said.

Jonah watched as Isis and Dr. Taylor stared at each other. She wished she could hear what he was thinking because she knew what Isis was thinking. Her sister had it bad for Dr. Tall-Dark-And-Handsome.

"Okay, I'll write her a prescription." Dr. Taylor said.

Dr. Taylor pulled a prescription pad from his pocket and began scribbling on it. He handed the prescription to Isis.

"You guys take care," he said before exiting.

"Okay, let's go and we'll get this filled." Isis said.

Isis left the room. Her sisters followed her out while Jonah changed back into her clothes.

Jonah walked across the roof and sat next to Isis She looked deep in thought.

"So, you and the doctor. What is it you called him? Dr. McDreamy?" Jonah teased.

"I never called-" she turned to look at Jonah. "Oh, God. You were listening to my thoughts?"

"Yeah. Sorry, can't help it." Jonah said. She turned back to look out at the sky. "You like him."

Isis didn't say anything for a while. It wasn't like Jonah really needed her to respond. She already knew the answer.

"Yeah, I do." She said after a while.

"Hmm."

"What?" Isis turned back to face Jonah.

"Nothing."

"See now that's not fair. You know what I'm thinking so tell me what you're thinking."

"I just never thought I would see the day when you fell for a guy."

"Ugh, me neither and I don't even know how it happened. I'm usually so careful. Sad thing is I don't know how he feels about me." She looked at Jonah questioningly.

"Sorry, can't help with that. I couldn't hear his thoughts."

"Really?"

"Yup. It's just you guys."

"That's a crappy power."

"Tell me about it."

They laughed. This was the first time they've laughed in the last few days. With all of this power stuff they haven't been able to find the funny.

"What are you two doing?"

Jonah turned around to see Genesis walking over to them. Freedom and Liberty were behind her.

"Oh, we're just taking about my very crappy mind reading power."

Jonah turned to look at Isis. *Thank you.* Jonah will respect her privacy. At the moment she hasn't put a handle on her feelings for Dr. Taylor so Jonah wouldn't say anything.

Genesis, Freedom and Liberty sat down beside them.

"I don't think your power is crappy," Liberty said.

"I can only hear your thoughts. Nobody else's."

"Really?" Freedom asked. "That kinda sucks."

"See, crappy. You guys got all the cool powers and I'm stuck with mind reading. Limited to my sisters."

"But that's not your only power. Mom said you would be getting another one. Maybe it will be better," Liberty said. She sounded so optimistic.

Little did she know, Jonah had already gotten that power and she wouldn't exactly call it cool. An annoyance maybe, but not cool. It was right up their with being able to read her sister's minds.

Chapter 14: Jonah

September 7, 2014

It was a new day and Jonah was glad to put everything that happened the day before behind her. Today she got to take her mind off of being a witch and be a bartender. Oh Happy Day.

She was working behind the bar when she got this urge to look up. To her surprise her sisters walked in. *So much for a normal day.* She didn't think she would ever get used to being able to sense them. She wondered if they could sense when she was near.

The hostess walked them over to a booth. Jonah stepped over to Danielle.

"Hey, Danielle, I'm going to go on my break," Jonah said.

"Okay," Danielle replied.

Jonah left the bar and joined her sisters. "I didn't know you guys were coming."

"We were all free so we thought we would stop by," Genesis said.

"How are you feeling?" Isis asked.

"I didn't have another attack," Jonah said.

"I wasn't-"

TaQuanda Taylor

"You were thinking it," Jonah cut her off.

"Guilty," Isis said. "But you can't blame me."

"I don't but I wish you wouldn't worry."

"Are you on lunch?" Genesis asked.

"Yeah."

A waitress walked over to them.

"Hey Jo, are you on lunch?" she asked.

"Yeah." Jonah said. She gestured to the table.

She waved at everyone. "I hate to ask you this but Tony just got here."

Jonah looked over her shoulder. Sitting at a table alone was a man. He had blond hair, glasses and he was looking down at his hands.

"Oh, damn," Jonah said. She forgot that he was going to be here.

"What?" Genesis asked.

"It's nothing."

"It's Jonah's regular." The waitress responded.

"Thanks a lot for that."

"Jonah's regular?" Isis asked. She looked over at the man.

"Yeah. He only comes in when Jonah is working and only lets her wait on him. Even though she's behind the bar now." She turned her attention back to Jonah. "I can try again but he won't even look at me."

"It's okay. Can you let them know to make Tony's regular and I'll come get it when it's done?"

"Sure." She walked away. *Finally.* Jonah didn't need her stirring up any more trouble.

"You're on lunch. Let someone else take care of him," Genesis said.

"It's fine. Besides, she was right. He really won't let anyone wait on him and I should have waited to take my break until after he got here."

"And that's supposed to make me feel better? I don't like the way he's looking at you." Genesis was staring at Tony.

Jonah noticed that they all were staring at him. She looked over her shoulder to see what the wonder was. Tony smiled when he caught Jonah looking. She smiled back and turned to her sisters.

"He's harmless."

"Okay, but you're still on lunch. Someone else can give him his regular," Genesis said. *There is something about him that doesn't feel right.*

"He's really alright. He's been coming here for years. There's nothing to worry about." Jonah addressed Genesis.

"Can you read his mind?" Liberty asked in a whisper.

"I don't think so. I haven't heard anyone's thoughts all day. Not until you guys got here."

"So you really can only read our minds," Freedom said.

"Seems that way."

TaQuanda Taylor

A different waitress walked over.

"Hi, my name is Lea, and I'll be your server." She notices Jonah's presence for the first time. "Oh, Jonah, I didn't see you there."

"That's okay Lea. We haven't looked at the menu yet."

"Okay, take your time. Just wave me over when you're ready. 'Kay?" Lea said.

"Yeah."

Lea bounced away.

Jonah leaned into the table so that no one except her sisters could hear her.

"Can you guys sense me when I'm near?"

"What do you mean?" Freedom asked.

"I mean, when you guys walked in here, I knew it before I looked up and saw you."

"Really?" Genesis asked.

"You guys don't have the same feeling?"

"I haven't noticed anything. We've been together all day and I knew you were here so I didn't need to 'sense' you." Liberty said.

"Yeah, that makes sense."

"Maybe this is the power mom was talking about." Isis said.

"It's not."

"How do you know?" Isis asked.

"I just do."

"Another feeling?" Freedom asked.

"Something like that."

"Sounds like a power to me." Liberty said nonchalantly.

"What, the über sensitive power?"

"There's a empathy power." Liberty said.

"How do you know that?" Genesis asked.

"I read it in that book I got." She answered. She turned to Jonah. "It's where you can pick up on feelings and things from other people."

"Maybe you're an Empath." Freedom said.

"Maybe." Jonah wanted to drop the conversation. She knew what her new power was and it wasn't empathy.

The first waitress walked back over to them.

"His order is all ready for you," she said as she walked by.

"I'll be right back. Look at the menu and order something before you guys get kicked out."

"They won't kick us out. Will they?" Freedom asked.

"No, they won't kick you out, but order."

"Jonah," Genesis said.

TaQuanda Taylor

"It's okay. I'll be right back." Jonah walked away before Genesis could protest further.

Jonah walked over to collect Tony's order and carried it over to his table.

"Hey Tony. Sorry to keep you waiting." She placed the tray on the table and sat his food in front of him. He smiled up at her.

"Hi, Jonah. I'm sorry, I didn't know you had company."

"Don't worry about it. It's just my sisters."

"Oh. They're all very pretty."

"Yeah, they're all right. I won't be replacing them any time soon."

Tony laughed.

"Oh, you know what? I forgot your soda. I'll be right back Tony."

Jonah turned quickly and bumped into a waitress.

Her chest tightened. She gasped for air. *It's happening again.* She tried to suck back in the air that was escaping her. She felt rather than saw the panic from her sisters. They raced over to her.

"Where's you inhaler?" Isis shouted at her.

Jonah couldn't answer her. It was hard to breath. *I need air.* She knew that it wouldn't do anything but she stumbled to the door. Rachel the hostess reached out for her. That single touch made her chest tighten more. *This really hurts.*

Jonah could hear Isis shouting at someone. "Where is her purse?"

Jonah made it outside and stumbled to the sidewalk. She was not thinking about where she was going. Her feet seemed to lead her. She couldn't see anything in front of her. Images were playing in her head.

There were people rushing by, many oblivious to what was happening to her. In their hurry, she was bumped into several times. Each time her breathing worsened.

She was trying to avoid being hit. She wanted this to end. Nothing in front of her was visible, just the images in her head. They changed every time a new person bumped into her.

A man rushed by and practically spun her around from the force of the impact. The images changed again. She felt like she was choking. *Please don't let me die.* She dropped to her knees and threw her hands out in front of her to stop herself from hitting the ground with her face.

The people on the sidewalk stopped and they were standing and gawking at her. Everyone from inside was outside.

"I called 911." Jonah could hear Lea say.

No.

She couldn't say the word out loud.

Her vision was becoming clearer. Jonah could see in front of her. Isis was waving something in front of her face, trying to get it closer. It was her inhaler. She reached out with shaky hands to push it away.

Her breathing returned to normal.

"Take the inhaler," Isis said.

"I don't need it."

TaQuanda Taylor

"Jonah, take the damn inhaler." Genesis said. She sounded worried.

"I'm fine."

Jonah sat back on her heels and steadied her breathing. She looked up into the worried and scared faces of everyone.

"I'm fine, everybody. Go back to whatever you were doing."

People slowly scattered away.

"Okay, this is more than some asthma attack. Something else is going on," Isis said.

"You're right, but we can't talk about it here." Jonah said.

Jonah could hear the sirens from the ambulance.

"I really wish she hadn't called them," Jonah said.

"We thought you were dying," Liberty said softly

Jonah turned to look at Liberty. *Why is this happening to me? Who up there thought that I could handle this?*

"Are you sure you're okay?" Liberty asked.

"Yeah." Jonah reached out and took her hand. She squeezed it reassuringly. *I hope I'm okay.*

Jonah sat on the back on the ambulance and let the two cute paramedics check her over. She felt bad that they came all this way for nothing. She looked up at her sisters. They were standing on the sidewalk huddled together. They were all watching her closely. Jonah wanted to scream at them that she was fine but she didn't. For a minute there even she had thought she was dying.

"Everything seems okay. Are you sure you don't want to go to the hospital?" Cute paramedic number one asked.

"I have the right to refuse, correct?"

"Yes."

"Then I refuse. Thank you so much."

"Okay, but next time, use your inhaler." Cute paramedic number two admonished.

"Yes, sir." He had no idea that the inhaler was useless to her.

Jonah jumped down and walked over to her sisters.

"See, I'm fine."

"I am going to choose to trust you." Isis said.

"Thank you.

"Can we go home?" Liberty asked.

"Yeah, I just have to go grab my things."

"I'll do it." Freedom said.

"It's okay, I can grab my own things."

"Just trying to help." Freedom said.

"I know and I thank you for that, but I don't want you guys to treat me like I'm going to break."

"Then maybe you should stop almost breaking. You're not the one with super healing powers remember?" Genesis adds.

"I remember oh powerful sister." Jonah said jokingly.

"I'm not joking," Genesis said.

"Okay, I'll try to stop almost breaking."

"Okay." Genesis said.

"I'm going to go get my things, you guys can go to the car."

They all turned and walked towards the car. Jonah turned to go inside and stopped when she saw Tony. He looked freaked out.

"Tony, I'm sorry if I scared you."

"I'm okay. Are you?"

"Yeah. I'm just going to go home."

"Oh. Okay. Yeah, me too."

He walked away quickly. Jonah shook her head. *Poor guy.* She turned and went inside to get her things and to let them know that she was leaving.

Chapter 15: Genesis

"*Premonitions?* Are you serious?" Genesis asked.

"As serious as me not being able to breath," Jonah said.

"Not funny."

"Sorry."

Jonah dropped a bombshell on them. She admitted that while she was having her asthma attacks, she was actually having a premonition. She had several today as a result of so many people bumping into her.

"They look painful." Freedom said.

"They are," Jonah replied.

"But why?" Freedom asked.

"I don't know. I didn't make up this power. You're going to have to ask the woman who did and while you're at it can you ask her why she thought I would want this?" Jonah said.

"Sure thing," Freedom said sarcastically.

"Okay, can we get back on topic?" Genesis asked.

Genesis was trying to wrap her head around the fact that Jonah had premonitions. Not to mention the fact that they looked like they were killing her in the process. Now was not the time to make jokes.

"What did you see?" Liberty asked.

"At first nothing. It was a bunch of random images, but then," Jonah hesitated. She looked like she was struggling to continue.

"Then what?" Genesis probed.

"Then some guy bumped into me outside and it wasn't random anymore. It was specific, very specific." She finished.

"What did you see?" Isis asked.

Jonah didn't say anything for a while. She looked up at Liberty.

"What did you see?" Liberty asked.

"I saw the man that bumped into me grab a girl." Jonah said.

"What do you mean you saw him grab a girl?"

"You know? Kidnapped. Abducted. He grabs her. I don't know how else to say it." Jonah said.

She got up from the couch and started pacing.

"What's wrong?"

"I don't want this. It's bad enough that I'm stuck with hearing your thoughts but now I get images of things that are going to happen? And then there's the issue on whether or not to do something. If we don't we put somebody in danger. If we do we're involving ourselves in something that is way outside of our scope." Jonah said.

"Maybe not?" Liberty said.

"What do you mean?" Genesis turned to look at Liberty.

"She got that premonition for a reason. I think it's clear. We can't ignore it, we have to do something." Liberty said.

"What you're saying is we have to stop this man?" Isis asked.

"Yeah. Isn't it obvious?" Liberty asked.

"I think it is." Freedom said.

"You two don't know what you're talking about."

"Why, because we're young? Somebody didn't think we were too young when they gave us these powers." Freedom said.

"But this is something that the police should do."

"Then let's call the police." Isis said. "There problem solved."

"That depends. What else can you tell us Jo?"

"Nothing."

"Nothing?" Liberty asked. "How? You can't see it anymore?"

"No. I didn't see it before." Jonah spoke softly. She looked defeated. "I could only see the mans face clearly. I couldn't even see the girl. I don't know what time it happens or where it happens."

"Well that sucks." Freedom said.

"Tell me about it." Jonah said.

"So, then we can't go to the police."

"Why not?" Isis asked.

"Because we have nothing to tell them. They can't just go into this blind."

"Okay, so if the police won't go in blind. Why do you guys think it's okay that we do?" Isis asked.

"Because I don't think we have a choice." Liberty said.

"But I think we do have a choice. The police." Isis said.

"I already told you we can't go to the police."

"But you're a cop, can't you use some pull to get them to listen to us?" Isis asked.

Genesis took a deep breath and looked around the room. She might as well fill them in on everything that happened Friday. There was no keeping it a secret now. Her gaze fell on Jonah. She looked at Genesis with understanding, no doubt reading her mind. *Here goes nothing.*

"I don't actually have much pull right now," Genesis said.

"Why?" Isis asked.

"I got suspended on Friday."

"What?" Isis asked.

"Why?" Liberty questioned.

"Are you okay?" Freedom wondered.

"Did you know about this?" Isis asked, looking at Jonah.

"I found out when you guys did. Well, actually a few minutes before," Jonah said pointing to her head.

"So explain. What happened?" Isis looked back at Genesis.

"It's just a precaution."

"Precaution for what?" Isis asked.

"The guy that she beat up," Jonah said.

"I did not beat him up."

"Hey, that's what you were thinking," Jonah said.

"What's going on?" Isis asked.

"Because I walked away Friday after that arrest without any serious injuries, and the guy is still in the hospital, I was suspended."

"They think you beat that guy up?" Liberty asked.

"No."

"I don't get it," Freedom said. "Why suspend you if they don't think you did anything wrong?"

"How many times have you guys shown me a video of some cop beating someone up?" Genesis didn't give them an opportunity to answer. "In case the guy wakes up and says that I used excessive force, they are trying to be one step ahead."

"So, they're trying to save their own butts," Isis said.

"Pretty much."

"So when do you go back to work?" Isis asked.

"I don't know but I don't want you guys to worry. It's going to be okay."

"Okay," Isis said.

"Okay?" Genesis looked at her skeptically.

"Yeah," Isis said. "I trust you."

Genesis looked around at the rest of them. They all nodded their heads in agreement.

"So, that means that we really are on our own with this." Isis put her head in her hands.

"Yeah, I think we are."

"So how do we go about this? What's our first move?" Liberty asked.

"Well, I think the first thing is for Jonah to think really hard about where this takes place. We can't do anything if we don't have a location."

Jonah looked down at her feet. "All I know is that it is in a park - a big one. Like Central Park or Marine Park. But I don't know which one."

"That's good. That gives us a starting point."

"But that doesn't really narrow it down." Isis looked up.

"It narrows it down enough."

"Okay, so we have a location. Rather two locations. Now what?"" Liberty asked.

"Since Jonah is the only who knows what this guy looks like. I think we need to know too."

"I could draw him. I mean if Jo tells me what he looks like." Freedom offered.

"That's actually a good idea. Normally we would use a police sketch artist. You're the closet thing we have to one."

"Jo?" Freedom asked.

"Sure, let's do this." Jonah walked towards the bedroom. Freedom stood from the couch and followed her in.

"Now what?" Liberty asked.

"I guess while they're doing that, we should try to come up with a plan."

"This is crazy." Isis stood and left the living room.

Genesis got up and followed her into the kitchen. Isis opened the window and sat on the ledge with a leg on either side.

"I really hate it when you do that?"

"The fire escape is right here. I'm not going to fall," she said.

"What's wrong?"

"It's just … this is our lives now, isn't it? This is what we are going to spend our time doing. Putting our lives in danger to save complete strangers."

"I don't know."

"I have so much more respect for you, right now."

"Why?"

"Because, this is what you do everyday. You never know what you're going to come across when you go to work. Just having to do this one job and I'm freaking out. I don't know how you do it."

Genesis pulled one of the chairs over to her and sat. "It's not that bad. So, why are you freaking out?"

"I don't know."

"Don't give me that. You're freaking out for a reason, so what is it?"

Isis looked out the window for a moment before she spoke. "Everything is happening too fast."

"You mean being a witch?"

"Yeah, and now this thing. We just found out 24 hours ago about this witch thing. We don't even know what all of this means. Are there more like us? Why didn't mom tell us? Why do we have powers? Where does this all come from? There is so much that we don't know. We shouldn't have to deal with all this. They shouldn't have to deal with this."

Genesis knew that she was talking about Liberty and Freedom.

"Believe me if I could shield them from this I would, but this is happening to them as much as it is happening to us. We weren't given a choice in the matter."

"Yeah. It seems that our days of having a choice are over."

Genesis turned to see Liberty walk into the kitchen.

"Are you okay?" she asked.

"Yeah." Isis answered.

Jonah walked in.

"What's going on in here?"

"Just talking. Is she done?"

"No. She kicked me out."

"Okay, so while she's working on that, I guess we should try to figure out how we're going to go about stopping this guy."

"Any ideas?" Jonah asked.

They all looked around at each other.

"Well, no one said this would be easy."

"Hence, the fact that I think we're out of our minds." Isis said.

"Ice, we get it. You don't want to do this. But right now I don't think we have any choice so unless you have something helpful to say, how about not saying anything at all?" Genesis didn't want to be mean but she was ready to move past Isis' objections.

"Okay, so what do we know?" Liberty asked.

"A guy grabs a girl in a park."

"We know that it may be either Central Park or Marine Park." Liberty said.

"What if it's neither?" Isis asked.

Genesis turned to glare at her. *All right already. We know you don't like this.*

"I'm not trying to be negative," she said, "not much anyway. I'm just saying, what if we get to these parks and check them out and he's not at either of them. Then what?"

"Then we fail." Jonah said.

They all sat quietly for a moment. The thought that some girl's life was in their hands and they could possibly fail was sickening. They didn't ask for this and yet it was given to them. Genesis was not in the business of failing.

"I trust Jonah, so if she said it's going to happen at either of those parks, then I don't think we'll fail." Genesis said. She noticed that Jonah looked away. Maybe she was also worried about them failing.

"This isn't going to work if we don't all think it will."

"They were alone." Jonah said.

"What?"

"When he grabs her, they were alone in the park. So, the first thing we have to do is make sure that they're not alone." Jonah answered.

"That sounds simple enough." Isis said.

"But how do we do that?" Liberty asked.

"We stay back." Genesis said. "We don't leave them alone but we don't get close enough that we put ourselves in danger."

"If he's not by himself with her maybe he won't be inclined to grab her." Isis said.

"Exactly."

"Okay. Yeah. That does sound simple." Liberty said.

"I'm done!" Freedom called from the living room.

They all stepped into the living room and Freedom held up her sketchpad.

"Is this him?"

Jonah stepped forward and looked at the picture. Freedom had added color to the picture to identify features Jonah told her about. He looked like a normal guy with red hair, blue eyes and a cleft chin.

"Yeah," Jonah said, "That's him."

"Yeah? I got him?"

"Yeah, that's him. That's the guy." Jonah said.

"Good job, Free," Liberty said.

"Thanks." Freedom beamed.

"Okay, now we know who we're looking for. Can you make some copies?" Genesis asked.

"Yeah," Freedom said. She walked over to the computer and printer sitting by the window.

"Okay, so which park should we check out first?" Genesis asked.

"I think we should split up." Jonah said. Genesis looked over at her. "I don't know what time this happens. We'll cover more ground if we split up," she said.

"Okay, how do we split up?"

"I think three of us should go to Central Park. It's a little bigger." Liberty said.

"That makes sense."

TaQuanda Taylor

"Isis, can you teleport more than yourself?" Freedom asked.

Chapter 16: Isis

"What?"

"Can you teleport anyone other than just you?" Freedom asked.

"I don't know."

Isis haven't even teleported on her own yet. *Why would she want to know if I can teleport others?*

"I'm asking because whoever is going to go to Marine Park can take the car and you can take the rest to Central Park." Freedom said.

"It would be easier than getting on the train." Liberty said.

"Well, I haven't even teleported on my own." Isis said, speaking her earlier thoughts. "I don't even know how to."

"You should be able to just think of where you want to be and then … just be there." Liberty said.

"It couldn't hurt to try." Genesis said.

"Especially since it's getting dark and we should be leaving." Jonah added.

All of her sisters were looking at her like they expected her to be able to do this. And what if she couldn't? *Will they be disappointed?*

"No, we won't." Jonah said.

Isis didn't think she would ever get used to Jonah being able to read her thoughts. Either way she might as well try this because they wouldn't let it go.

"No, we won't." Jonah said.

"Please, stop that." *Here goes nothing.*

Isis couldn't believe how nervous she was. She closed her eyes and took a deep breath to steady herself. She was really nervous. The few times that she had managed to teleport she hadn't been trying to. It was something that just happened. She thought back to the first time she had teleported. Then she had thought that she was suffering from blackouts. Now, here she was trying to make herself teleport.

Isis took another deep breath. She thought about her room. *Oh, how I wish I was there right now - Away from all of this craziness.*

Her body suddenly felt weightless. It was a weird yet comforting feeling. She opened her eyes to tell her sisters what she was feeling. She let out a gasp.

Isis was standing in her dark bedroom.

"Whoa. It worked." She had to admit that this was really cool.

"Time to get back." She closed her eyes again and thought about the living room. The familiar feeling of being weightless returned. Isis now knew that she was teleporting. She opened her eyes.

"That was so cool." Freedom gushed.

"Did it work? Did you end up where you wanted to?" Genesis asked.

"Oh yeah. It worked."

"Okay, now try to take someone with you." Liberty said.

"Me, me, me. Take me." Freedom held her hand up like she was in class waiting to be picked to answer a question.

"Please take her before she jumps out of her skin." Genesis said.

"Okay. Come on."

Freedom bounced over to Isis. Isis held her hand out and Freedom took it.

Isis closed her eyes and thought of the kitchen this time. She felt the weightlessness of her body but then it stopped. Instead she felt heavy.

She tried again.

Again, the feeling of being heavy followed the feeling of being weightless.

Isis opened her eyes. Maybe she couldn't teleport with anyone. Jonah walked over and stood in front of her and Freedom.

"Close your eyes." Jonah said. To Freedom she said. "Freedom, think about going to the kitchen. Isis, try again."

Isis took a deep breath and thought about being in the kitchen.

She felt weightless. This time the feeling of being heavy didn't follow. Isis opened her eyes and they were standing in the kitchen.

It worked.

She looked at Freedom. Her eyes were squeezed shut.

"Freedom. Open your eyes."

She opened one eye. Her mouth dropped open and the other eye popped open.

"Can we please switch powers?" She asked in amazement.

"Absolutely not." Isis was just beginning to like this power.

"This is so cool."

"Let's go back." Isis took her hand.

"But it's right there."

"What fun is that?"

Freedom beamed a smile that showed her age. Isis wished she didn't have to go through this. She closed her eyes. Isis didn't have to tell her to think about the living room.

Isis opened her eyes and they were back in the living room.

"I take it that it worked?" Genesis asked.

"Yes!" Freedom exclaimed.

"Okay good. We should be leaving." Liberty said.

"Let's hope it'll work when you take two people." Genesis said.

"Oh, it'll work."

"Liberty and I will take Marine Park." Jonah said.

"Okay, so the three of us will take Central Park."

"Okay, we're gone." Jonah said.

Jonah headed to the door and Liberty followed.

"We'll conference call when we're in place." Genesis said.

"Got it." Jonah said.

Jonah and Liberty left the apartment. Isis walked over to the window and watched while they exited the building, walked over to the car and drove off. She walked back over to Genesis and Freedom.

"Let's do this."

"Are you nervous?" Freedom asked Genesis.

"A little." Genesis answered.

"Just think about Central Park."

Isis took their hands and closed her eyes. When she opened her eyes they were standing at the 81st street entrance.

Chapter 17: Liberty

Liberty walked around her area of the park in silence. She was conferenced in with her sisters but no one was speaking.

Once everyone was in place. Genesis had called Isis. Isis called Freedom and synced the two calls together. Freedom called Liberty and synced her two calls and Liberty called Jonah syncing her two calls.

Now they were all synced in together. They've been here for about twenty minutes and nothing's happened. What if Isis was right and they were not in the right spot?

"So, anybody got anything planned this week?" Jonah asked.

"Are you seriously talking about what we're doing this week?" Isis asked.

"What? Are we supposed to just walk around silent and bored?" Jonah asked.

"If we're going to talk about anything, how about a certain someone turning seventeen next month." Genesis said.

"Yeah. Let's talk about that." Jonah said.

"We should have a party." Isis said, giving in.

TaQuanda Taylor

"Do I get a say?" Freedom asked.

"It's your birthday, so yeah." Isis said.

"Where would we have the party?" Freedom asked.

"At the house." Genesis said.

"How big of a party are we talking?" Freedom asked.

Her sister's talked about Freedom's upcoming birthday but she couldn't join in on the conversation. Liberty was too busy staring at the man who had just entered the park.

She looked down at the sketch and back up. She was staring at the man in the picture.

"Well, it's your party so how big do you want it?" Jonah said into the phone.

"Hey guys." Liberty tried to get their attention.

"I don't know. The apartment's not that big," Freedom said.

"We could have a roof party," Isis said.

"Guys." Liberty tried again.

"I don't know. I think I would be too worried about kids falling off of the roof," Genesis said.

"Guys!" Liberty yelled as quietly as she could.

"What?" Jonah asked.

"He's here."

"I'm coming." Liberty could hear Jonah running.

"Isis, get Freedom and then come get me," Genesis instructed.

Liberty lowered the paper and looked around.

"We're alone." She tried to speak so that only her sisters could hear.

Realization hit her as she looked around. She was the only girl there.

Her eyes stopped on the man. He was looking right at her. Liberty turned her back on him and dropped the paper with his image. She needed to get out of there and away from him.

She shut off her phone and put it in the inside pocket of the hoodie she was wearing. She was trying to act casually as she walked away. Liberty could hear him getting closer behind her.

She didn't want to think about what might happen. He's got to be after somebody else.

Jonah said she didn't see the girl's face. Surely she would have said something if it was her. Wouldn't she?

She could feel him behind her. Liberty started to move a little faster. Where is Jonah?

ISIS

Jonah ran into the clearing where Liberty was waiting. Isis stood alone in the area. She bent and picked up a piece of paper. It was the sketch of the man.

"She's gone." Isis said.

Jonah had her chance to pace earlier now it was Isis' turn. They were back at home with no idea of where Liberty was.

TaQuanda Taylor

When Liberty's phone went dead, Isis had teleported from Central Park to where she was in Marine Park, but she was too late. The only thing that was left was the picture she had of the man they were looking for. Isis knew this whole thing had been a bad idea.

"I don't understand how Liberty got grabbed."

"Because it was her." Jonah said.

Isis stopped pacing and turned to look at her. Genesis and Freedom were glaring at her.

"The girl in my vision was Liberty." Jonah continued.

"You said you didn't see the girl."

"I lied." Jonah said.

"What? You lied to us?" Genesis asked. "Why would you do that?"

"Because if I told you the truth you would have made Liberty stay home. You would have made all of us stay home."

"Of course I would have," Genesis said.

"But that would have been wrong. Liberty needed to be in that park," Jonah said.

"You knew what park it was going to happen in?" Isis asked.

"Yes," Jonah said.

"You lied to us." Genesis said again.

"Yes. I lied to you. I can't explain it right now, but I had to lie." Jonah said. "What we need to focus on right now is getting Liberty back."

"She wouldn't be missing if you had told us the truth."

Jonah turned to look at Isis. Isis hoped that she was listening very closely to her thoughts. Isis hoped that she was hearing how pissed she was at her.

"I get that you're mad at me. Believe me. If the roles were reversed I would be mad too but right now we need to focus on Liberty. You can be mad at me later." Jonah said.

"I'm pissed that you think you can tell me when to be mad."

"No secrets, remember? Or did you forget what that means?" Genesis asked.

"No I didn't forget what that means. I already said I don't know how to explain why I couldn't tell you the truth." Jonah said.

"Maybe you should try."

"Would you guys stop?" Freedom asked.

They all turned to look at her.

"While, we're sitting here trying to figure out why Jo lied to us, our sister is sitting God knows where. I think we need to focus on that." Freedom said.

"Freedom is right." Genesis said.

"Is there anything else you're not telling us?" Isis asked.

"No." Jonah answered.

"Then how are we supposed to find her?"

"When we do get her back, I say we all go and get tracking devices implanted in us. That will make it a lot easier." Freedom said.

Isis stopped pacing. She couldn't believe that she didn't think of it before. When she had tried to get to Liberty before she was thinking about the park. They didn't need a tracking device. *I should be able to get to Liberty. All I have to do is think about her. Right?*

Her eyes locked onto Jonah's. Jonah was looking at Isis with understanding. She cupped her mouth with one hand to hide what she mouthed to her "go". *More secrets, huh?* Jonah dropped her hand. Isis didn't have time to question her now. She needed to get to Liberty.

Isis looked around the large basement she was standing in. It was dark but oddly warm. Liberty was lying in the middle of the floor. She looked like she was sleeping. Isis dropped to her knees near her.

"Liberty, wake up."

Someone made a sound and it was not Liberty. It was a mix between a groan and a whimper. Isis looked up and let out a gasp.

There was a pretty large cage near the end of the basement. Packed inside were girls. They were sitting or lying on top of each other. The sound came from the girl near the front of the cage. She was bound, gagged and staring right at Isis. *I need to get Liberty and these girls out of here.*

There was a sound above them. Footsteps. Isis searched Liberty until she found her phone. *Good girl.*

The basement door opened. She dashed across the basement and hid behind a chair. She could hear the man descending the stairs. Isis powered up Liberty's phone. She got into the settings and turned on the hotspot. Isis connected her phone to Liberty's hotspot and sent a text message.

Freedom's phone signaled that she had a new message. She took the phone out and looked at the message.

"Yes." She said excitedly.

"What is it?" Genesis asked.

Freedom handed the phone to Genesis while she got up to grab the laptop.

"Find my iPhone?" Genesis read the message.

"She wants me to track her phone." Freedom said.

"Can you do that?" Genesis asked.

"If she connected to WIFI, yeah."

"Okay. You do that and I'll call in reinforcements." Genesis took out her phone and left the living room.

Isis could hear the man moving around in the basement. His shoes were scraping along the floor. She hoped Freedom got her message. Isis silenced her phone in case she tried to text back. She tried to put Liberty's phone in her pocket. It slipped out of her hand and hit the floor.

Crap. Please let him be deaf.

161

TaQuanda Taylor

Not a chance. He reached behind the chair and took her hair in his hands. He pulled and yanked her from behind the chair.

"Ah!" *This really hurts.*

Isis fell to the floor beside Liberty. The girl in the cage was whimpering. *Honey, I know how you feel right now. I should have teleported out with Liberty but I'm not sure it would have worked with her being unconscious.*

"How the hell did you get here?" He said through clinched teeth.

Isis was not really sure how to answer that. *What do I say, the truth? I mean, the girl saw me teleport in but would he believe it?*

Isis stole a peak to her right and Liberty was staring at her. *Oh, Thank God she's okay.* Isis mouthed "no" to her. The last thing she needed right now was for Liberty to let this man know that she was awake. Liberty closed her eyes. *Good girl.*

The man walked over and took Isis' hair in his hands. *What is it with him and pulling my hair? He's worse than a girl in a girl fight.*

No time to think about that. He used her hair to pull her to her feet. Isis could barely recognize the scream that was coming from her.

Isis tried to fight him off and scratched him across the face. He screamed out in pain and let go of her hair. He punched her and she could feel her nose break. The pain was too much; she didn't even realize that she was screaming

While she was clutching her nose in agony he hurled her across the basement. *God, will this ever end.*

Chapter 18: Genesis

"*What* you are asking me is impossible?"

Genesis stared at Lieutenant Prado from across his desk. All she wanted right now was for him to rescue her sisters. Instead he was sitting very calmly across from her, denying her.

"What happened to we protect our own? Am I no longer considered part of the team?"

"If you are asking me if you have been fired, then the answer is no."

"Then why can't you do this?"

"Because as part of the team you know that we have procedures that we have to follow. Now you can report your sisters to missing persons and once they have been missing for twenty-four hours then the necessary steps will be taken to find them."

"We can't wait twenty-four hours. We need to find them now. There isn't much you need to do. We have a location we just need a team and a warrant so we can enter the premises."

"And how are you sure that your sisters aren't in their on their own free will? Or that they're even in there?"

"I can't tell you that." Genesis stood up and placed her hands on his desk.

"Well you better tell me if you want me to go breaking protocol for you."

She dropped her head. *Maybe I should tell him. What's the worst that could happen? He could think I'm crazy and officially dismiss me from my job. Right now my job isn't that important my sisters are. Here goes nothing.*

"My sister has premonitions. She had one today of a girl being grabbed in a park. We split up and tried to prevent it from happening. He grabbed Liberty instead." *There. It wasn't telling him the whole truth but it was telling him enough.*

"Why didn't you call 911 when you learned of a possible abduction?" *What?* He didn't even flinch when she told him that she had a sister who had premonitions

"I didn't think anyone would believe me."

"So you knowingly put yourself and your sisters in danger?"

"Can we please discuss my parenting skills after we get my sisters back?"

"I thought he only grabbed one?"

"He did. Isis tracked down Liberty and now we need to get them both back."

"If Isis was able to get to your sister then how come she can't get them out?"

"I don't know!" Genesis didn't mean to yell but she could feel her anger starting to boil over.

"Tell me how you got the location again?"

"Isis texted Freedom and told her to track her phone using Find My iPhone. She did and that was how we got the location."

Lieutenant Prado picked up a pen and began writing on a pad on his desk.

"Look. If you don't want to help me ... help us." Genesis pointed outside his office to Jonah and Freedom huddled together. "Just let me know and I'll go get my sisters myself. I can't make any promises that I'll be following any procedures of the job. What with me being suspended and all."

Lieutenant Prado looked past her and out the window at her sisters.

"Which one is the psychic?"

"The one with the Hooters uniform on." Genesis just noticed that Jonah hadn't changed out of her uniform. With everything that happened after she had her premonition she probably forgot.

"I want to speak to her."

Genesis walked over to the door and opened it. She motioned for Jonah to come here and for Freedom to stay put. Jonah entered the office and she closed the door.

"What's your name?"

"Jonah." She answered.

"Genesis tells me that you're a psychic and that you had a premonition tonight. Tell me about it."

Genesis held her breath while Jonah repeated, almost verbatim, what she's told Lieutenant Prado. She sent up a prayer to God, thanking him for Jonah's ability to read her mind. If her story had been different Genesis didn't know what he would have done.

TaQuanda Taylor

He picked up a card from his desk and handed it to Jonah.

"If you have anymore premonitions you call me. You understand?"

"Yes sir." She said.

He picked up his phone and dialed a series of numbers. "Give me a minute."

They turned to leave his office. Before Genesis closed the door behind her she could hear him talk into the receiver. "Judge Roberts. Sorry to bother you. I need a warrant to search a home."

Again. Thank you God.

Chapter 19: Liberty

Liberty woke up feeling groggy. It took her a moment but she managed to get her eyes open. It was dark and hard for her to see. She tried to sit up but her limps felt really heavy. She relaxed back and closed her eyes. She tried to remember what happened. Then she heard a noise.

She thought her mind was playing tricks on her and then she heard it again. Isis screaming. There was a thud to her right.

Her eyes shot open and she looked over. Isis was on her stomach next to her. Liberty saw fear and then relief flash in her eyes. Isis mouthed "no" and Liberty closed her eyes. She made sure to leave them open a slit so that she could still see what was going on.

The man walked over and took Isis' hair in his hands. He pulled, lifting her to her feet and she let out another scream. Liberty held her breath. It was hard watching her sister be attacked.

Isis tried to fight him off. She scratched him across the face. He let her go and screamed out in pain. Isis didn't have enough time to get away. He recovered quickly and punched her in the face.

Liberty cringed. She knew without a shadow of a doubt that he had broken something. The sound was easily heard in the quiet basement and Isis' screams of agony let her know it was true.

The man grabbed Isis and hurled her across the basement. She landed somewhere over Liberty's head. The man walked over to her. Liberty opened her eyes and turned her head so that she could see them.

Isis lay on top of a table. It looked like the type of table that you would find in a morgue.

The man stood in front of her and wrapped his hands around her neck. Isis struggled in his grasp.

Liberty looked away because she didn't think she could take seeing any more. She saw a small trashcan sitting beside the table. There appeared to be something inside of it. She prayed that there was.

She had the power for the elements but had only been able to manipulate water. She should also be able to manipulate Fire, Air, Earth and Spirit.

Liberty thought now was as good a time as any to try to conjure fire.

She turned her head away. She wasn't sure of what the first step in calling an element was. She remembered how the element was called in one of her favorite books and she closed her eyes.

She took a deep breath and called fire. She asked it to show itself to her. She was practically begging for fire to appear.

Liberty felt her body warm. Soon it felt like it was on fire. The added heat didn't burn it actually felt comfortable.

She heard a gasp come from the direction her feet were pointed and opened her eyes. Her vision glowed the color of burning flames. She raised her head and looked down at herself. The feeling of being on fire wasn't just a feeling. She actually was on fire. Her entire body was covered in flames. It was incredible. She had never experienced anything like it before.

She would have taken more time to admire the new feeling but she heard something clatter above her. She turned her head and watched Isis flailing about on the table.

Liberty pulled her attention away and focused on the trashcan. She imagined cupping some of the fire that consumed her. She threw her arm out at the trashcan. It immediately caught fire.

The man noticed the fire and let go of Isis. He grabbed the trashcan and rushed over to a sink sitting in the corner. Isis lay on the table in a heap. Liberty prayed that she was still alive. Liberty thanked fire and asked it to leave her. It obeyed.

She turned on her side and looked at the man at the sink. He was trying to get the trashcan under the running water.

"No," she whispered. The water stopped. "More." The flames in the trashcan increased.

The man screamed and tried not to drop the trashcan. Liberty felt Isis next to her. She turned back to her sister. There was blood running from her nose.

"Are you okay?"

"I think my nose is broken," Isis struggled to say.

"We need to get out of here," she said.

Isis tried to help her stand but she was in pain.

"I can stand on my own."

Liberty got to her feet and then bent to help Isis to hers.

"Do you think you have enough energy to teleport us out of here?" Liberty asked.

TaQuanda Taylor

"We can't go," Isis breathed out.

"Why not?"

Isis struggled to raise her arm. She pointed across the room. Liberty followed her aim and her mouth fell open.

She now realized where the gasp she had heard earlier had come from. She stared into the eyes of a young girl who couldn't have been much older than she was. The girl was in a cage with other girls. They were packed really tightly together.

"Jonah said you were the girl in her vision."

"I know."

"She said you were supposed to be in that park."

Liberty looked at the girls in the cage.

"To get them out of here."

Liberty started to maneuver Isis towards the large cage. Isis screamed out and fell to the floor. Liberty turned to see that the man had abandoned the trashcan and had knocked Isis down.

Liberty didn't have time to react. He backhanded her and she stumbled into a pillar. He had his hands around her neck choking her as he had choked Isis.

Liberty began to panic. She was a small girl and he was a big guy. If Isis hadn't been able to get him off of her than she had no shot.

She struggled to loosen his grip, fighting to breath. She heard the girl bang on the cage and remembered that there had been a gasp when she had called fire to her. The girl had seen it happen. Weird time to think of that now.

The fire had not affected her and she knew how to call it back. She hoped that the fire would affect him. She didn't want to hurt him but she did want him to let her go.

She tried calling fire to her but it felt as if his grip had tightened. She could no longer think about calling fire. The only thought on her mind was breathing.

Liberty heard sirens outside. The man heard them too and turned his head. His grip loosened and that gave her the opening she needed. She called fire to her. She remembered what it felt like when the flames had covered her body and she welcomed that feeling.

She felt her skin warm up and the man must have too because he turned his attention back to her. It didn't take long for her body to be engulfed in flames. The flames wrapped around his hands and began snaking up his arms. He screamed and let her go. He ran over to the sink.

Liberty dropped to her knees and grabbed her neck, gasping for air. The flames left her without her asking them to. She looked over at the man and saw that he was struggling to get the water on. As much as she wanted too she knew she couldn't let him burn.

Turn on.

The water obeyed her. He shoved his hands and arms under the water.

Liberty crawled over to Isis. Isis was lying in a ball, holding her nose crying. Liberty could see the blood seeping between her fingers.

Liberty removed her hoodie and tried to put it against Isis' nose. Isis cringed against the pain.

"You're a nurse. What would you tell me to do?"

"Try and stop the bleeding," Isis groaned.

"Okay, so stop the bleeding."

Isis allowed Liberty to help her hold the hoodie to her broken, bleeding nose. Liberty looked over and saw that the man had almost put the fire out. Liberty couldn't let the fire go out. She was afraid that no matter how much damage had been done to him he would come after them. She asked the flames to leave his arms but to simmer on his hands.

There was a sound from above.

"We're down here!" she called out.

The door to the basement opened and officers descended the stairs, guns drawn.

Thank you fire. You can leave.

The flames went out and the man dropped to the floor crying in agony. Liberty was sure he would have third degree burns. It was something she couldn't think about. She turned her attention back to her sister.

Liberty walked outside of the house behind Isis' stretcher. Genesis, Jonah and Freedom ran over to them. Liberty practically collapsed in Genesis' arms.

"I don't think I've ever been more happy to see you," she said. Liberty turned her attention to the paramedics. "Can you give us a minute?"

"We have to get her to the hospital," one of the paramedics said.

"It's okay," Isis said.

"All right, but make it quick." The paramedics walked away.

"What happened to you?" Genesis asked.

"She has a broken nose," Liberty answered.

"Are you okay?" Jonah asked.

"I'll be fine," Isis said. She looked at Genesis. "I could really use that healing power of yours."

"I wish I could share it with you," Genesis said.

Genesis took Isis' hand. Liberty caught the look on Jonah's face. It was pure shock.

"What?" Liberty asked.

"Ice, tell them," Jonah said.

"I'm not in pain anymore," Isis said.

"What's going on?" Freedom asked.

"Genie just took her pain away," Jonah said.

"I did?" Genesis asked.

"Yeah," Isis responded.

"Everybody's doing new things today," Liberty said.

"What do you mean?" Freedom asked.

"I conjured fire," Liberty said.

"Really? How? What was it like?" Freedom hurled questions at her.

"My entire body was covered in flames," Liberty said.

"Is that what happened to that guy?" Genesis asked.

"Yes. He had his hands around my throat. I think he's going to have third degree burns."

"What? He choked you?" Genesis asked.

"Yes, and can I say that us Battle women are going to have to work really hard on not being strangled."

The paramedics returned. "We have to take her now."

"Okay," Genesis said. "We're right behind you."

The paramedics carted Isis away.

"Oh, I think someone saw me catch on fire," Liberty said.

"What?" Genesis asked. "How could someone have seen you?"

Jonah turned towards the ambulance and then to them.

"Someone saw Isis teleport in," Jonah said.

"How do you know that?" Liberty asked.

"She told me," Jonah responded. Jonah pointed to her head.

"I don't get how someone could have seen you. Was it that guy? I'm sure no one will believe him," Genesis said.

"No, It wasn't the guy," Liberty said.

One by one girls were walked out of the house. Many were taken to waiting ambulances and others were taken to police cars. Liberty counted fifteen girls.

"OHMYGOD," Freedom said.

"It was dark. I didn't see which girl it was," Liberty said.

"We have to clean this up," Genesis said. "Nobody should know about us."

"Freedom, go with Isis. We'll meet you guys there," Jonah said.

"Okay," Freedom ran off to the ambulance before it pulled off.

The girls went to do damage control and make sure that the girl who had seen both Isis and Liberty use their power would remain silent.

They were unaware of the fact that they were being watched.

Chapter 20: Jonah

Jonah stepped into the visiting room. She stared at the plastic box that would be containing her mother. She felt butterflies in her stomach. This was the second time that she had been here to see her mom and the first time that she had come alone.

She opted not to tell her sisters what she was planning to do. She and Eve needed some one on one time because they had some things that they needed to discuss.

She hated keeping things from her sisters. It especially seemed unfair because she was able to pry into their thoughts but they had no idea what she was thinking. It wasn't her fault though. She had not asked for the ability to hear her sisters thoughts, it had been given to her.

At some point she knew that she would have to tell her sisters about the premonition she had had in the parking lot, but first she needed to get answers.

She took a deep breath and walked over to the plastic box. She took one of the five waiting stools and faced her mother who was already inside.

"I was wondering when you were going to be back," Eve said. "You have your power of premonition."

"Yes," Jonah said.

They suddenly fell into an uncomfortable silence. Jonah felt like she was staring at a stranger. There was very little about the woman sitting in front of her that felt like her mother. She was sure that it had a lot to do with the fact that she hadn't seen her in years.

"If there is something you want to ask me, ask," Eve said.

"You can read my mind, right?" Jonah asked.

"Yes."

Jonah took a breath and thought about her very first premonition. The one she had while leaving the prison the first time. She let her mind wander back to the images that had accompanied her breathing attack.

The images flooded her mind.

She was entering a small room with her sisters. There were four rows of chairs and strangers occupied them. In front of them was a window with the curtain drawn. The curtain opened.

Jonah stared at her mother through the thin plastic.

"Is it true?'

Eve looked down at her hands and Jonah felt like the air had been ripped from her lunges. It was a different feeling from her premonitions but it was still uncomfortable. Eve had just confirmed the premonition without ever speaking.

"Look at me," she managed to say.

Eve looked up and met her eyes.

"OHMYGOD!"

"Please relax," Eve said calmly. It was actually too calm for Jonah.

"Relax? How can you ask me to relax?" she asked. "You're going to be executed?"

Saying the words out loud made it too real for her. In the ten years that her mom had spent behind bars she never thought that she would ever say anything like it. Jonah had just thought she would always be here, in this place.

When she had had the premonition she had almost decided to ignore it. Although she had the ability to hear her sister's thoughts and her mother had said that she hadn't gotten her true power, being able to see something from the future just didn't seem real.

It didn't seem right that her first premonition would be of her mother dying. It wasn't until she had the series of other premonitions, including the one of Liberty being grabbed, that she knew she couldn't ignore this one.

Now having confirmation that this was real was almost too much to handle.

"Yes, I'm going to be executed," Eve said, breaking through her thoughts. "But I had my moment and now I'm over it and you should be too. This is how it's meant to be."

"But I haven't had my <u>moment</u>. Wait. How long have you known?"

"From the moment I sensed your powers on you."

"What does that have to do with anything?"

"I should have told you girls about this sooner but I never thought that it would get to this point. I never <u>wanted</u> it to get to this point."

"Ma, what are you talking about?"

TaQuanda Taylor

"In order for you girls to get your powers, I have to…"

"Die?" Jonah finished.

"Yes."

"I don't understand."

"It's like a stipulation set on our powers centuries ago. The child does not get her power until the mother ceases to be no more."

"But you're still here."

"Yes. But my execution is already set in stone."

Hearing her mother tell her this made her fell worse. She felt like this whole thing was her fault. She had been given this amazing gift, although it mostly felt like a burden, and now her mother was going to die because of it.

If her and her sister's didn't have their powers their mom would still live. It was a fact that made having these powers more difficult. Add on top of that the fact that she had been angry and had avoided her mom for ten years.

She should've been to see her more and now she wouldn't be able to get that time back. She hated herself and wouldn't be surprised if her mom hated her.

"I don't hate you."

"Why not?" Jonah wiped her hand across her face.

Her hand was wet. She hadn't realized that she had been crying. She looked down at her shirt and it was coated with her tears.

"Do me a favor."

Jonah looked up and saw that Eve had placed her right hand on the plastic.

"Put your hand up here."

Jonah raised her left hand and placed it against her mom's.
"Now close you eyes and take a deep breath."

Jonah did as she was instructed. She wasn't sure what was going on. Then she felt the room drift away.

Eve walked quickly down a dark alley. It was softly raining.

"You can't run from me, Eve!"

She whirled around and stared at the man behind her. He was aiming a gun at her. She looked up at the sky and made the rain fall harder. She looked back at him and he squinted against the rain.

"You know what will happen if you kill me."

"It's a price I'm willing to pay."

Eve watched him pull the trigger and teleported so that she was standing behind him. He turned to try shooting again. She flicked her wrist and he went flying across the alley and crashed on top of a large blue garbage can. She turned to run from the alley but had a moment of weakness. She turned back to see if he was okay and found him siting up. He fired the gun again.

She threw her hand up to stop the bullet. It faltered for a moment and then turned. The man fell over. She knew that she should have gotten out of there but she had to make sure that he was okay. She wasn't a killer. That would be the final mistake she would make that night.

TaQuanda Taylor

She approached him and attempted to take his pulse.

"Freeze!"

She whirled around to face two police officers.

Jonah opened her eyes and stared into her mother's.

"Now you know the truth."

"What? That you're dying because of an accident. Was that supposed to make me feel better?"

"It was supposed to answer all of the questions that you've wanted to ask for years."

"But it doesn't make this any better."

Her tears were falling harder.

"I know it doesn't. But it's all I have right now. All I can do is tell you that I'm going to be okay."

"Who was that guy?"

"It's not important."

"No. What it is; is not fair."

Eve and Jonah kept their hands pressed against the plastic barrier. Jonah's head dropped as she sobbed.

Someday the loss of me will lesson and you will be left with all of the good memories.

Jonah's head shot up and she stared at her mother through her tears. A few days ago she would have had no idea what she had heard. Now she had grown used to hearing thoughts and was now able to tell the difference between a thought and a voice.

"I can hear your thoughts."

"That's because you dropped that wall you had up around yourself regarding me. You're letting me in."

"I'm so sorry. I'm so sorry." Jonah cried.

You have nothing to be sorry for. Eve.

But I abandoned you. Jonah.

No. I abandoned you. Ten years ago I should have stayed in New York and not come to Philly. Eve.

It wasn't your fault. Jonah.

And this is not yours. Eve.

Jonah sat, cried and listened to her mother's voice. It was only in her head but it felt good. A few days ago she would have never admitted to missing her mother. Now she could hear her thoughts.

Chapter 21: Aftermath

Genesis, Isis, Liberty and Freedom sat around the living room. Chinese food containers sat on the table in front of them. Freedom scooped rice onto her plate.

"Where's Jo?" Isis asked.

"I don't know. She asked to use the car this morning." Genesis answered.

"She didn't say where she was going?" Liberty asked.

"No, and I didn't want to ask out of fear of her lying to me again." Genesis said.

"You're not going to let her live this down are you?" Freedom asked.

"I can't be the only one who feels like they can't trust her anymore?" Genesis asked.

"I trust her just fine." Isis said.

"She lied to us." Genesis said.

"Yeah but she had a reason." Liberty said.

"And her reason put you and Isis in danger," Genesis said. "I can't believe I'm the only one who remembers that."

"Believe me," Isis gently touched her bandaged nose. "I remember it, but while I was in the hospital I thought about it. She had no choice but to lie to us."

"Unbelievable," Genesis said.

"If you took a second to think about it you would get it too. You're just so upset about the fact that she lied, that you can't see the whole picture." Isis said.

"I'm thinking about the picture." Genesis said.

"No, you're thinking about what happened to me and Lib. Think about those fifteen girls that were in that basement, because I'm sure Jo was when she made that call." Isis said.

Genesis looked around the living room at her sisters.

"You all feel like I'm overeating?"

"Knowing Jo as well as I do, I can safely assume that it bothered her keeping the truth from you. I also know that if she knew that those girls were there and that the only way to find them was with Lib and Ice, that she would have done what she needed to do." Freedom said.

"And I know that if she had told you everything that you would have called off the whole thing and those girls wouldn't be back with their families." Liberty added.

"So now I'm the bad guy," Genesis said.

"No one is saying that you're the bad guy, we're saying that you should give Jo a break. She only did what she felt she had to do." Isis said.

"She gets a lot of those feelings," Liberty said.

"Do you guys think she's more powerful than us?" Freedom asked.

"Why would you ask that?" Genesis asked.

"In just a few days, she can already do more than us. I'm thinking when we really get the hang of this, she's going to be pretty powerful." Freedom said.

They all looked around at each other.

They had all thought that this was even ground. They thought that they each possessed one power. Yet, Freedom was right. Jonah wasn't limited to just one power.

Jonah stepped out of the car and walked towards the apartment. She had stayed away a little longer to ensure that the puffiness in her eyes went down. She didn't want her sisters to suspect anything. She hated lying to them but she had made a promise to her mom not to tell them what was going on.

The news that Eve would soon no longer be physically there was too much for her to bare and if she could give her sisters a little more time before they would have to deal with it then so be it.

For the time being she would keep her mom's secret.

Jonah stopped on the bottom step of the stoop. The hairs on her arms were standing up.

Someone was watching her. She was sure of it. She slowly turned around and peered into the dark. She looked around but didn't see anyone.

Whoever it was, was keeping his distance.

She didn't know why someone would be watching her.

Jonah turned and ran up the stoop and into the apartment.

"Try not to watch her so closely." Eve stepped into the shadows and stood beside a man.

"She can't see me," he replied.

"Yeah, but she's not like the other girls. She'll know you're there, every time. When she's around, try to stay farther back." Eve turned to look at the man. "This isn't like watching them when they had no powers. Everything is different now."

"Everything is what you were afraid of." He said. He turned to look at Eve. His face hidden by a hoodie. "Does she know everything?"

"She knows what she needs to know. She doesn't know about you, which is why I need you to stay back."

"I'll stay back."

"I have to get back."

"She'll see you again?"

"Yeah."

"You got what you've always wanted."

"Yeah and all it cost me was my life."

Eve stepped up to the man and kissed him lightly on the lips. He placed his hand on her face.

"Will I see you again?" he asked.

"Until death do us part."

The man was standing in the shadows alone. He took one more look at the house before he turned and left.

THE END... FOR NOW

TaQuanda Taylor

BE ON THE LOOKOUT FOR BOOK TWO IN THE FIVE SISTERS SERIES...

About The Author

TaQuanda Taylor was born in Rochester, New York in 1985, the oldest child of James Hawkins and Crystal Taylor. She has eight younger siblings between her father and mother. TaQuanda attended high school at Rochester's School of the Arts. She attended Full Sail University for college where she earned her Bachelor of Fine Arts in Creative Writing for Entertainment in 2014. TaQuanda lived briefly in Brooklyn, New York before settling back in Rochester.

Stay In Touch

Website: www.taquandataylor.wordpress.com
Facebook: www.facebook.com/TaylorTaQuanda
Twitter: www.twitter.com/TaQuandaTaylor
Google+: https://plus.google.com/u/0/107458744863168732212
Amazon: amazon.com/author/taquandataylor

Join my newsletter and receive a special gift about this series.
Newsletter: http://wordpress.us9.list-manage.com/subscribe?u=1f156096f3a3f1c352095071e&id=55a591ba3f

A Note From The Author

Hey guys if you made it this far I want to thank you so much for reading my very first book. I had a blast writing this story and I hope that you had a blast reading it. I can't wait to bring you the second book *The Five Sisters: Revealed.* It would mean the world to me if you would stop by my website, Facebook page or Amazon to leave a review about this book.
Again, thank you so much.
Much Love, Peace & Chicken Grease.